DOUBLE DEATH

Mrs Farland is a wealthy widow who insists that she is being poisoned. Is this true, or is she a hypochondriac with delusions? Her suspects vary, and she keeps altering her will. Her solicitor, Walton, engages a professional nurse, who in due course arrives and is swiftly poisoned. This opening episode, setting the scene, is by Dorothy L. Sayers. Now it's up to her five successors, each of them a distinguished writer of detective fiction, to develop the plot in whatever direction they think fit. This book is a winner on at least three counts: as a splendid whodunit; as a delightful period piece; and as a highly revealing insight into how the minds of the great detective story writers work.

DOUBLE DEATH
A Murder Story

by
Dorothy L. Sayers
Freeman Wills Crofts
Valentine Williams
F. Tennyson Jesse
Anthony Armstrong
David Hume
Supervised and with a Preface
and Prologue by John Chancellor

A Lythway Book

CHIVERS PRESS
BATH

First published in Great Britain in volume form
1939
by
Victor Gollancz Ltd
This Large Print edition published by
Chivers Press
by arrangement with
Victor Gollancz Ltd
1991

ISBN 0 7451 1386 9

British Library Cataloguing in Publication Data available

NOTE

In preparing this book for press, certain minor Editorial modifications were made in the various contributions in order to make the story a straightforward and consecutive narrative. Thus no author should be held entirely responsible for the contribution which appears under his or her name.

CONTENTS

PREFACE

The responsibility for this book, which gives an authentic glimpse into the unguarded minds of six different authors, rests upon James W. Drawbell, Editor of the *Sunday Chronicle*, and William Lees, Feature Editor of the Allied Newspapers.

It was Drawbell who conceived the idea of publishing a murder story to be written by six different authors, each author to contribute a separate chapter, and Lees who got it done.

As each author completed a chapter the growing manuscript was handed on to the next man or woman, with the blessings of Lees and Drawbell and the notes supplied by the various authors for the guidance of their successors.

At the end of it all I was appointed to be the 'All-Seeing Eye of God', so wistfully hoped for by Miss F. Tennyson Jesse in the notes to her chapter.

It was my job to straighten things out, and a good deal of straightening out was necessary, for each new brain as it approached the task had set off in a different direction from that followed by its predecessors.

One or two of the authors would not permit their manuscripts to be altered (although none objected to cutting), and that did not make things any happier for the 'All-Seeing Eye', particularly as some of the authors were ignorant of, or indifferent to, the peculiar needs of newspapers.

Eventually the 'All-Seeing Eye' hit on the plan of writing a prologue to the story. This allowed the tail of the cat to protrude from the bag, but it linked up Dorothy L. Sayers' beginnings with David Hume's solution, and therefore it has been allowed to stand.

The authors' notes are published here exactly as they were written, except that deletions have been made of arguments or suggestions dealing with parts of the story which the 'All-Seeing Eye' deemed it necessary to remove.

When the authors wrote their notes they did not know that their trust might be violated and the workings of their minds shown naked to the world, as is here being done.

The responsibility for that rests with David Hume, who suggested it, and Victor Gollancz, who approved the suggestion.

JOHN CHANCELLOR

PROLOGUE

by *John Chancellor*

'Give me the other pillow, Millie,' said Mrs
Farland peevishly. 'Then take the tray away
and fetch my port. And why aren't the evening
papers here yet?'

'Yes, Aunt Emma,' Millie said, in the tone of
one breathlessly anxious to please. 'I don't
know why they're late . . . Oh, dear, where did I
put that pillow? . . . Perhaps the train was late at
Yowle, or perhaps the boy's had a puncture . . .
Oh, here it is! . . . Now lift your head. There! Is
that better?'

'Nothing's ever better,' said Mrs Farland.
'Open the curtains. Why should the place be
like a tomb? Let some air in.'

Millie rushed to obey, and Aunt Emma
Farland, sitting up amidst her silken pillows,
looked on maliciously.

Even now, after weeks of illness, Aunt Emma
was a striking and commanding figure. When
she looked, in the mirror, at her rouged cheeks,
scarlet fingernails, mascara'd eyelashes and
henna'd perm, she liked to think that nobody
could guess her to be forty-seven; and one of
her private bed-games was to compare her
physical attractions to the detriment of Millie's.

1

Millie, with her straggly brown hair always escaping from its bun, her slim figure in its faded jumper, her cotton stockings, the white scar on her forehead, her ever-crooked pince-nez, and her general air of twittering incompetence, had never, Aunt Emma frequently and loudly declared, had any sex-appeal at all, nor ever would; and that obvious fact was a source of great satisfaction to Aunt Emma, whose sex-appeal in the past had been something to reckon with, and was, she thoroughly believed, as devastating as ever.

'There!' said Millie, that being one of her favourite expressions, and having drawn the curtains and twittered uselessly round the room a couple of times, she came to the foot of the bed to smile at Aunt Emma. 'Now I'll fetch your port and see if the papers have come, and you'll be comfy for the night.'

'No I shan't,' said Aunt Emma, who could never forgive Millie for being only twenty-two years old, even though she made so little of her youth. 'I'm much too ill to read papers and the port will make me sick again, and of course it's your evening out.'

'Yes, Aunt Emma,' Millie agreed meekly.

'What possible pleasure you can derive from tramping down to the village on a winter night is beyond me. But I suppose you find something to do at the Institute.'

'Yes, Aunt Emma.'

'Well, run along and do it then!' Aunt Emma exclaimed with sudden violence, and she smacked her blue-veined hands on the silk counterpane. 'Don't stand there smirking at me like that. Send the maid up with the port and the paper and get along, or else you'll be saying I never give you any time to yourself.'

'Oh, no, Aunt Emma, I'd never say that. You're always so kind.'

'Get out!' said Aunt Emma.

Millie hurried down the dark staircase of the old country house, the flat heels of her loose shoes flapping on the oak treads, and went to her room.

It was a curious room for a bed-chamber. It was at the end of a draughty and unfrequented corridor on the ground floor. Aunt Emma, having too much conscience to put her niece up amongst the servants, and too much jealousy to let her sleep on the same floor as herself, had given her that room as a compromise.

Millie made a light and locked her bedroom door. Then, although it was cold in there, because a large french window gave on a disused conservatory filled with mildew and empty flowerpots, she stripped herself naked.

She hung a fluffy and most un-Millie-like negligée round her shoulders, sat in front of her chipped white-painted dressing-table, let her hair out of its bun, and brushed and waved it.

She did these things with the air of a woman

3

who is conscious and proud of her body. Seen now, unclad, it was a body which no woman need have been ashamed of.

Presently she rose again.

From beneath her mattress she removed a key and unlocked a cupboard door.

The cupboard was filled with clothes on hangers, and it had two shelves, on one of which was a row of hats and on the other a large selection of crêpe-de-Chine lingerie and silk stockings. At the bottom of the cupboard was a row of shoes with three- and four-inch heels.

Changing from her workaday clothes into her secret finery had a curious effect on Millie.

In casting off her shapeless jumper, bulging corsets and cotton stockings she cast off, too, all that was known of Millie in Whitestones.

Her twittering anxiety to please, her squirming inferiority complex, her visible incompetence in everything, fell from her as if they were garments as ugly as the rest.

When she drew on her silk stockings, and stretched her white arms into a crêpe-de-Chine slip, and looked at herself again, she was a different woman.

She was a woman of the world, with poise and personality. Most miraculous of all, she was a woman with charm.

Half-dressed, she sat in front of her glass again and used lipstick, rouge and powder. Her face, if not beautiful, became mysteriously

4

arresting. Her brown eyes grew deep and lustrous; her full sensual lips mobile and inviting. The scar on her forehead ceased to be a blemish and changed into the outward symbol of a strange inner glamour.

When she was fully dressed she put out the light, pulled back the curtains, unlocked the french window, and went out through the musty conservatory into the garden.

No one saw her go. No one ever did.

She crossed the garden, dark and damp. She crossed the paddock, and emerged in the lane. From there she could see the lights of the car waiting at the top, and she hurried along.

The near-side door of the car swung open as she arrived, and the driver, leaning across the passenger's seat, stretched his hand out towards her.

'Millie, darling!' he said.

'Oh, Jim, dear!'

There was no Millie-twitter in her voice when she spoke to him. It was a clear, rich, lovely voice, tender and thrilling.

She entered the car and he put his arms round her. They kissed, and drew back to look at each other in the glow of the dashlights. Her face wore the solemn expression of a woman in love as she traced the line of his clean-shaven jaw with her fingertips, and then drew him to her passionately again.

'Where shall we go tonight?' he asked at last.

'London?'

'There isn't time, sweetheart. Let's go to the roadhouse again and dance.'

'You're the most exciting woman in the world,' he said, and kissed her hand. 'I could dance with you for ever.'

She cuddled close to him, and he started the car and drove away.

PART ONE

by Dorothy L. Sayers

I

It was tiresome of Mrs Farland to insist that she was being poisoned. Her illness, with its odd, variable symptoms, did indeed appear to puzzle Dr Cheedle; but doctors are puzzled more frequently than the lay person supposes, and Dr Cheedle's partner, Dr Parry, said roundly that in his opinion these alternations of abdominal pain, sickness, vertigo, insomnia, sense of suffocation, and so forth were pure hysteria. Always arbitrary and suspicious by nature, Mrs Farland was now undoubtedly getting 'queer'; but this latest development of a sort of 'persecution mania' was highly inconvenient, to say the least of it.

It would have made things easier if Mrs Farland could have made up her mind which member of her household to accuse. Her first selection, of course, was poor Millie Pink. Millie had been her Aunt Emma's companion and butt for several years—ever since she had had to give up school-teaching. Her aunt said it was no wonder Millie's health had given way under the persecutions of the Upper Fourth;

you had only to look at her to see that she was incapable of maintaining discipline. Why, even Li-Ho the Peke defied her. To do the flowers, write letters to her aunt's dictation, comb Li-Ho and convey household orders to servants who despised her was really all she was fit for, and a salary smaller than the cook's wages, far more than she was worth. After all, she had a comfortable home at Whitestones, and Mrs Farland had promised to remember her in her will. It was the recollection of this promise that now suggested peril to Aunt Emma. She hinted from time to time that Millie would be glad to get rid of her, and, since this inexplicable illness had come on, had several times accused her of trying to poison her for her money.

Mr Walton, the solicitor from Creepe, had accordingly been instructed to alter Mrs Farland's will. But, though the alteration was publicly announced, Mrs Farland got no better, and her suspicions shifted to John Farland. John was twenty-seven, the son of the late Mr Farland's younger brother who was killed in the War. His uncle had adopted him and shortly afterwards died, leaving his widow to cope, unwillingly, with this cuckoo in the nest. Not that there were any native nestlings for John to oust, for the Farlands were childless. Mrs Farland objected to him because, out of her husband's estate, £15,000 were secured to him after her own death—an arrangement which

8

robbed her of a good deal of power. In the meantime, she enjoyed sole use of the life-interest, on condition that she provided 'suitably' for John. This she had done by sending him to the cheapest Oxford College she could find, and thereafter wangling him a job as assistant-manager in Farland's, the manufacturing chemists at Creepe. Mr Farland had sold out his interest in the firm when he retired in 1920, but the name, of course, still carried weight, and John's expectations made it worth while to overlook the fact that he showed no natural talent for a business career. The job carried more prestige than pay; but then, he could live with his aunt at Whitestones, travelling each day to Creepe by the local train from Yowle, and so save board and lodging.

John had seemed contented enough till about a year ago; he had then suddenly announced: first, that he was engaged to Penelope Cheedle; secondly, that he was sick of walking half a mile twice a day and had bought himself a small second-hand Austin. These Bolshevik activities caused Mrs Farland to think that he was only waiting for her death in order to make ducks and drakes of his inheritance, and that, since the secret poisoner did not appear to be Millie, it was probably John.

The remedy seemed to be to remove John from Whitestones, and Mrs Farland reluctantly agreed to find, and pay for, his board-residence in Creepe. John made no objection: he was nearer to his work and his Penelope and freed from the rather melancholy atmosphere of Whitestones. But Mrs Farland was none the better.

Her suspicions (after hovering playfully about the head of the cook, who was sacked without beneficial result) then focused themselves upon Dr Cheedle, who, naturally, wanted to get rid of her in the interests of his daughter Penelope. This made the situation very awkward. Dr Parry was thrice suspect—as Dr Cheedle's partner, as having shown himself unsympathetic, and as being a young man of Socialist opinions who would be ready to poison any rich widow out of sheer malice. There was no other doctor in Creepe, and the man at Plunton (the nearest town in the other direction) was ruled out, because Mrs Farland had already quarrelled with him before transferring herself to the care of Dr Cheedle.

II

It was during the first week of January that Mrs Farland's illness suddenly became so much worse. Dr Cheedle and Dr Parry could not deny its seriousness. Poor Millie appeared to be worn out with nursing, and the patient, between her bouts of pain and sickness, became so violent and abusive and so wildly insistent that she was being murdered, that by the Saturday morning it was evident that something had to be done. Mrs Farland refused to hear of a nursing home—alleging that there was a conspiracy to 'put her away'. At length, Mr Walton (summoned to re-make Mrs Farland's will in favour of Millie, who was momentarily in favour again) suggested that, in the interests of all parties, a professional nurse should be engaged, 'someone with experience of mental cases'.

'Unfortunately,' said Dr Cheedle, 'we are very short of nurses with all this influenza about. I have four nurses engaged on critical pneumonia cases, and Nurse Brown has had to go to Nettlebury to attend a bad septic infection—'

'Besides which,' put in John Farland, with his impudent and rather attractive grin, 'all your nurses are probably in collusion with you to bump Aunt Emma off.'

'My dear boy,' said Dr Cheedle, offended, 'you must not say that kind of thing, even in jest.'

'But Mrs Farland may say it,' said Mr Walton. 'I understand that these—ah— eccentric patients have to be humoured. I was wondering; suppose I were to ring up my son—he is in practice, you know, in Harley Street—and ask him to send a reliable and experienced nurse. As a matter of fact, he may be coming to me for the week-end. If that would suit you, Doctor, I think I might be able to persuade my client to accept the situation. For the moment she still seems to retain some confidence in my integrity.'

'If you can obtain that,' replied Dr Cheedle, 'I can have no possible objection. Any nurse recommended by Dr Walton would be quite satisfactory. I must confess that these new symptoms puzzle me. If the patient shows no improvement by Monday, I shall ask for a consultation. Let me know, Mr Walton, if you succeed in making the arrangement. In the meantime, we must ask Miss Pink to carry on, with such assistance as our excellent district nurse can give her. I will look in again this evening to see if the new treatment has produced any improvement.'

So saying, he departed, looking considerably dissatisfied, while the solicitor returned upstairs to deal with his difficult client.

III

'So Walton's fixed it up all right,' said John. It was a quarter to two on the Sunday afternoon, and he had run over in his car to make inquiries.

'Yes,' said Millie Pink. 'Dr Cheedle rang up

12

this morning to say he had heard from Dr Walton that he was sending a very good nurse. Dr Walton is staying here with his father.'

'I know, Cheedle rang me up, too. Nurse Ponting is the name.'

'Ponting?'

'Yes—like the drapery stores.'

'Oh, of course.' Millie blushed and looked confused. 'I thought—so silly of me—of course, that must be the connection. She's getting in at Yowle by the 5.47.'

'That's the train that leaves Creepe at 5.24. I might pick her up and run her out,' said John, who had no opinion of the local train from Creepe Junction to Yowle, and felt that everybody must prefer his Austin. 'I say, Cousin Millie, have you had any rest at all?'

'Oh, yes, thank you. Aunt Emma seemed really much more comfortable during the night. She slept quite well after those cachets Dr Cheedle gave her—I was able to doze off several times. And Nurse Cran is relieving me for the whole afternoon. So good of her.' (Miss Cran was the district nurse.)

'Well then,' said John, 'if you don't want to lie down or anything, you'd better let me run you over to Creepe for this musical doings. How about it?'

Millie, who did not feel excited about the Creepe Church Choir's coming performance of the *Hymn of Praise*, hesitated:

13

'I don't know whether I *ought*—'

'Of course you ought. Freshen you up and do you good. Besides, if you're afraid to leave Aunt Emma to Crannie for a few hours, your behaviour will look pretty sinister. It's your last chance, you know, to drop a spot of poison in the Benger's before the Ponting female arrives.'

'Oh, John! how can you talk like that about your poor aunt?'

'Do stop pretending, Millie. Aunt Emma's always been a beastly bully to both of us, and you know it. Come on. Stick your hat and coat on, or we'll be late. I'll drop you at the church and toddle round to take Penelope out for a run. Shall I fetch you back with Nurse Ponting or will you have tea at the vicarage and wait for the 6.30 bus?'

He felt that tea at the vicarage would be a tempting thought to Millie—the vicar and his wife were always so kind—and then, Mr Johnson the curate might be there, who was always so polite and attentive and really so good-looking for a middle-aged man.

'It's a long time to leave poor Nurse Cran alone with poor Auntie,' Millie said.

'It's time you considered poor Millie, don't you think? I'll tell you what. Your show will be over before five. If you want me to run you back, drop round to Dr Cheedle's—I'll be there. If you don't come by a quarter past, I'll take it you've succumbed to the attractions of the parsonage.' And to this arrangement Millie, not without protests, agreed.

IV

Creepe Junction was a dreary little station, some fifty miles from London, on the main line between Yarborough and Haynes. Many expresses ignored it altogether, for Creepe itself, apart from the Chemical Works, was of no great importance.

At half-past two on this particular Sunday—just about the time that John Farland was depositing Millie Pink at the door of St Sebastian's Church—a stoutish woman in nurse's uniform alighted from the London train at Creepe Junction. In one hand she carried a suitcase; in the other, an umbrella and the little bag usually associated with her profession. Tom Tadman, the foreman-porter on duty, advanced upon her—not very hopefully, since the suitcase was small and not much could be expected from a nurse. Still, she was the only passenger with luggage of any sort, and it might be worth twopence to her to have it carried up the stairs. The nurse, however, clinging firmly to all her belongings, inquired for the train to Yowle.

'Yowle?' said Tom, shocked that anybody should want Yowle at a time so inappropriate. 'Nothing to Yowle till 5.24. You've been thinking of the old 3.3.' He spoke with a kind of affection, as though the train had been a boyhood friend. 'She was taken off, ah, a matter of five years ago and more.'

'I don't know anything about five years ago,' said the nurse, sharply. 'I was told to come by this train. How far is it to Yowle?'

'Ten miles or so by rail; a bit more by road. Quite a tidy bit more, if you was thinking of the bus—that goes round by Hopperton, you see.'

'There is a bus, then?'

'Yes,' said Tom, 'there's a bus all right. Only,' he added disappointingly, 'she don't go till 4.30. Tell you what; you best run out and get yourself a cup of tea or summink in the town. They'll be just about shutting the bars, of course, but you could sit down comfortably in the parlour at the Eagle or the Silver Cross—or the Temperance is handy and very respectable. You give me your bags and I'll leave 'em in the booking-office for you, so you can pick 'em up there if you wants to catch the 4.30 bus. She stops just outside the yard. I'll be about to see you gets them.'

'I suppose that's the best I can do,' said the nurse. She let Tom carry her suitcase up the stairs, where Jolly, the booking-clerk, was doing ticket-collector's duty; he noticed that she was booked through to Yowle, and that the company would therefore lose nothing by her transference to the bus. Mr Jolly obligingly

16

agreed to look after all her luggage and deliver it to her, if required, at 4.30. The small bag, however, she declined to part with.

'I'd better have it,' she said. 'We have to carry drugs and things about, you know, and we'd be blamed if the wrong person got hold of them. Not that anybody would, of course, but I shouldn't feel quite comfortable.'

The clerk agreed, pleasantly, that one couldn't be too careful with drugs. The nurse fished out three coppers for Tom, observing that if she wasn't there by 4.30, she would be catching the 5.24.

'Right you are, miss; I'll be looking out for you.'

As the passenger, bag in hand, was struggling with the elastic band that secured her umbrella, a man in a gold-laced cap came through the door from the bridge, crossed the little booking-hall, and went out into the station-approach.

'Is that the station-master?' asked the nurse, carelessly. The elastic was being tiresome, and she was forced to set down her bag and betake both hands to it.

'That's right,' said Tom. 'Off to his dinner. There ain't nothing now till the 5.9 up, barrin' the goods, that is.'

'Good-looking man,' remarked the nurse. She advanced to the doorway and opened her umbrella, while Tom restored the little bag.

'Most ladies think that,' replied Tom, with a wink. 'But you're too late, miss. He's married, is Mr Spiller. Got spliced in Haynes afore he came here.'

She frowned: then made up her mind to take the familiarity in good part.

'They always *are* married—the good-looking ones.'

'Yus,' said Tom. 'I'm married meself, come to that. Now see! The Temperance is just at the corner on the right, but if you wants the Eagle or the Cross you'll have to go into the town.'

'Thank you.' The nurse started off. Then she turned back and recalled Tom.

'By the way—can you tell me where Dr Cheedle lives?'

'Number Seven, Market Square. You can't miss it. The house with the big white porch, only two doors off the Eagle.'

The nurse thanked him and set off again. Tom Tadman watched her flapping cloak as it passed through the entrance, turned downwards, and was lost in the greyness of the falling rain.

V

John Farland was disappointed. When he reached No. 7, Market Square, he found nobody on view but the doctor. Penelope, said

18

Dr Cheedle, was out.

John said he would call back, and explained, rather guiltily, that he had made a provisional arrangement to meet Millie Pink at the doctor's house.

Dr Cheedle didn't seem too pleased about that.

'Oh, all right,' he said. 'Look in about a quarter to five. I've let the maids go to this church musical affair, but I can give you a cup of tea. So long.'

The dismissal was unmistakable. There now seemed little for John to do except to go to his own rooms and knock down the next two hours or so as best he might. He got into the Austin and turned its bonnet homewards.

VI

It was the noise of the 4.30 bus grinding up the approach to the station that reminded Tom Tadman of his passenger. He ran up the stairs, but the booking-hall was empty. Jolly, screened from interruption by his closed booking-window, was doing some clerical work in the far corner of his office.

'Hullo!' said Tom, popping his head round the door. 'Did that there nuss turn up for her bag?'

'I haven't seen her,' replied the clerk. He

19

added up a column of figures and wrote down the result. 'The bag's still there,' he went on, as though it might have been spirited away.

'Well, she's missed the bus.' Tom glanced out across the approach. It was very dark, and the rain was now falling implacably, splashing and dancing in the light from the lamps and windows of the bus. He came back. 'Nice day to dawdle round in, I *don't* think.'

Jolly, uninterested, started to work on another column, but broke off to ask:

'Who was that went over the bridge just now?'

'When?'

'About ten minutes ago.'

Tom shook his head. 'Dunno. I was in the lamp-room. I should think it was the Chief. I see him go into his office just as I come across.'

'Didn't sound like him. It was a heavy step, and he always walks light and quick. I stuck my head out when I'd finished putting these files away, but I couldn't see anybody. It might have been Willis or Langley.'

'They were both in the goods store. I'll have a scout round. But I expect it was Mr Spiller.'

Tom turned and went downstairs again. Privately, he felt convinced that nobody had come in but Mr Spiller. However, he glanced up and down the platform, opened and shut the waiting-room doors, investigated the lamp-room and the retreat labelled 'Gentlemen' and then crossed the line and did the same on the up platform, on which were situated the closed refreshment room, the closed book-stall, the station-master's office, the telegraph-room and the luggage lift. None of these yielded any marauder or wandering drunk or any person except Mr Spiller himself, who was seated harmlessly in his own domain, examining some waybills. The Ladies' Waiting-Room was dark and empty. In the General Waiting-Room, dimly illuminated by a single 25-watt lamp, the fire had nearly gone out; Tom charitably gave it a poke and threw on a couple of knobs of coal. There was nothing else remarkable to be seen except, on the chimney-piece, a flat glass flask of the kind supplied by whisky-distillers for convenient carriage in the car or coat-pocket. It was Black Horse Whisky of quarter-bottle capacity, and quite empty. Willis, the porter, whom Tom encountered as he left the waiting-room, said he thought it might have been left by the gent who travelled up by the 11.40; he had 'looked rather that sort'. He (Willis) hadn't noticed it when he glanced into the room after the train had gone, but there—it wasn't very big and he might have overlooked it. The flask was of no value; Tom dismissed it from his mind and embarked on an animated argument about football with Willis and Langley the shunter, while awaiting the arrival of the 5 o'clock from Plunton.

VII

When John called at a quarter to five, Dr Cheedle explained that Penelope had not yet come back. The doctor was a widower, and was making tea for himself with a caddy of Earl Grey's Mixture, a miniature Chinese tea-pot and a spirit-kettle. He was particular about tea, and never left it to the servants.

'Servants,' said the doctor, 'have no feeling for tea. Cheap Indian left stewing on the hob till it's the colour of old tawny boot-polish is what they like—and then six lumps of sugar to take away the bitterness. I keep that sort handy to revive lachrymose patients, but you and I know better, eh?'

John, who had never ventured to tell his future father-in-law that he really preferred 'sergeant-major's tea' to the most costly of China flavours, smiled sheepishly and accepted a second cup.

'It's a marvel to me,' pursued the doctor, 'how working-class stomachs stand it. Nice cupper tea first thing, tea for breakfast, tea for elevenses, tea after their dinner, tea, and tea for supper—they ought all to suffer from theine poisoning.'

'I should have thought nurses were the worst. I know, when I had my appendix out, I got the

22

notion that no nurse would refuse tea at any hour of the day or night.' The doctor grunted, and John went on: 'I think I may as well pick up this Nurse Ponting at the station and take her over to Whitestones. It's a foul evening for a drive, but it'll save her that half-mile at the other end. It's too bad that Aunt Emma won't allow the car out in bad weather. It's a dashed nuisance for visitors, not to speak of poor old Millie. She doesn't seem to be turning up, by the way.'

The doctor, who had opened his mouth to speak, took out his watch instead, and then opened the sitting-room door.

'The maids seem to have come in,' he observed, 'so Miss Pink should have been here by now.'

'I'll push along, then. The train is usually well on time.'

Two minutes in the car brought John to the station at 5.18. He helped himself to a platform ticket almost at the same time as a hefty young man in mufti, whom he recognised as one of the local constables. P.C. Bratton was, in fact, on the way to meet his young woman, who was returning from Yarborough by the London train due in at 5.20. Her name was Joan Fletcher, and she was an assistant in the most refined and imposing of Creepe's three hairdressing establishments. She was a smart young woman in every sense of the word, and

P.C. Bratton considered himself a lucky man, being due for promotion and hoping shortly to get married on the strength of it.

At the foot of the stair the two men encountered Tom Tadman, who greeted John with a touch of the cap and Bratton with a grin and a 'Watcher, Joe?' He had brought down the nurse's suitcase, and it now stood waiting to be taken across to the branch platform in company with that of any other passenger who might wish to proceed by the 5.24 to Snigthorpe, Nettlebury, Cobling, Yowle or Plunton.

For a Sunday evening, the 5.20 was rather full. P.C. Bratton, having spotted his Joan in the fore-part of the train, and obligingly lent his stalwart arm to extricate from the same compartment a very fat, lame woman carrying a small sack of potatoes, three cabbages in a strong bag and a bunch of chrysanthemums ('from me brother's allotment at Yarboro'— doin' well, Joe, thank'ee kindly'), found himself and his young lady in the rear of the little procession that trailed along towards the bridge.

Immediately in front of them was Willis, burdened with a heavy suitcase and a bag of golf-clubs. At the foot of the stairs stood John Farland, looking a little bewildered.

'Lost your party, sir?' inquired Bratton, with a smile.

'Yes, I can't make it out. It's a trained nurse for my aunt. She ought to have come from

London by this train. Most tiresome.'

'Nurse?' said Willis, overhearing. 'Why, there was a party of that sort come off the 2.32, booked to Yowle. Tom Tadman's got her bag over there on the branch. Would that be the lady you was looking for?'

'Must be, I suppose,' said John. 'What on earth made her come by that train? I meant to meet her and run her home.'

'Train's due out in sixty seconds,' said Willis. 'If the nurse is aboard, sir, you've time to catch her, if you sprint for it.'

'Confound it!' said John. 'Let her walk the other end.' On second thoughts, however, he sprinted. On the branch platform was Tom Tadman, carrying a case and glancing along the carriage windows in search of the owner.

'Hey!' cried John. 'Seen anything of a nurse in uniform?'

'No,' replied Tom, 'that's just what I ain't. This here's her bag. Blest if I know—'

The station-master, approaching from the direction of the van with the staff under his arm, was appealed to. He had seen no nurse; nor yet had Langley, who now came along, slamming doors as he passed. The train was signalled out. Tom embarked upon an explanation. At that moment, a woman came hastily out of the Ladies' Waiting-Room and ran full-tilt into the little group of men.

'Oh, the train's gone!' she cried. 'Oh, dear!

25

Porter! Oh, somebody's ill in there! Oh, dear me! Oh, John!'

'Good heavens, Millie,' said John, 'what are you doing here?'

'Oh, I changed my mind. I—oh, it doesn't matter! But there's somebody there in the cloakroom, groaning and making a terrible noise. Oh, dear!'

The men rushed in. In one corner of the waiting-room was a door leading to what Millie delicately called the cloakroom. From within came the sound of heavy breathing—stertorous and unnatural. John, without more ado, hurled himself against the door.

'I'll fetch the key,' said the station-master.

'I'll climb over the partition,' said Langley, with more commonsense.

Millie Pink, kneeling down, gasped: 'Oh, it's a nurse! It must be Nurse Ponting! I can see her cloak under the door.'

'Run, Tom,' Spiller said urgently. 'Tell them to phone for the doctor. She looks pretty queer. I'll open the door for you.'

'Sooicide?' demanded Langley, with relish.

'If Joe Bratton's still up there,' said Tom, 'I'll send him down.'

He set off at a run, and John seized hold of Millie, who was clinging to the door-handle, and led her out into the waiting-room.

In the meantime the door had been got open and the other two men were dragging out the helpless body of the nurse. She appeared to be sunk in a profound stupor; her face was swollen, and no shaking or pinching produced any sign of life in her. Her limbs swung heavily and inert like those of a corpse, and her slow, laboured and rattling breath reminded John of a patient in the last stages of pneumonia.

The station-master peered closely at her. 'Good God!' he said. 'I don't like this. How did she—?' He stopped abruptly as Tom Tadman ran in with the constable. 'Oh, Bratton,' he said, 'here's a nice thing. Passenger fallen down in a fit.'

P.C. Bratton shook his head. 'Maybe,' said he. 'Looks more to me like she'd been taking something. Doctor's job. Where did you find her? In here?'

He dived into the cloakroom and came out carrying the nurse's little bag. It opened easily. He searched the contents with an expert hand and eye, and was rewarded by the discovery of a small cardboard box, labelled in pencil, in block letters: 'SLEEPINE. 8 CACHETS. $1^{1}/_{2}$ GR.' He held it up. 'What's this? Sleepy stuff, isn't it?'

'Good lord!' cried John, 'I should think so. One of the barbiturates, and a dashed powerful one. It's on the first part of the Poisons Schedule.'

'Ah!' said Bratton. He opened the box. It contained a solitary white cachet.

27

NOTES

Possibilities of Development

I. Mrs Farland

(*a*) Her mysterious illness may really be due to
poison. If so, there are motives for:
1. Millie Pink.
2. John Farland.
3. Dr Cheedle (alone or in collusion).

The officious interference of Mr Walton
the solicitor in the matter of the nurse may
also have a sinister significance. Dr Parry is
a less likely suspect. (Nurse Cran and the
servants are still remoter possibilities. They
are introduced only by allusion, and Nurse
Cran was probably *really* at Whitestones all
Sunday afternoon.)

In this case, the motive for getting rid of
Nurse Ponting would be to prevent
discovery, and it might be desirable to
polish off Mrs F. on the Sunday evening or
Monday morning.

(*b*) The illness may be merely hysterical. In this
case, its importance will be only to confuse
the issue and (1) to bring Nurse Ponting
into the story; (2) to provide a source of
supply for the Sleepine. (See note on
Sleepine.)

28

II. *Millie Pink*

(*a*) She was a science mistress at school and knew something about chemicals, etc.

(*b*) She appeared startled by the name of Nurse Ponting, though she turned this off.

(*c*) Was she present *all the time* at the musical service?

(*d*) How did she come to be in the waiting-room at 5.24?

(*Note*: If innocent, she *may* have suffered some disappointment in connection with the curate, and preferred to go home by train rather than face John's chaff.)

III. *John Farland*

(*a*) He worked at Farland's and had access, no doubt, to the drugs there.

(*b*) He had a car (handy for conveying drugged people).

(*c*) He is just old enough to have known Nurse Ponting five years ago or more. Did she know of some youthful indiscretion of his?

(*d*) Is John, in fact, as amiable and easy-going and well-behaved as he appears? Has he ever raised money on his expectations?

(*e*) His insistence on fetching Nurse Ponting on so unpleasant a day may be kindness or design. If Penelope had not been out, would that have interfered with any plans he had? Or did he know beforehand that she would be out? (The doctor's servants were at the church and he may have seen them when he

29

dropped Millie.) Did he ever really intend to see Penelope?

(f) What was he doing between his two visits to Dr Cheedle's?

IV. Dr Cheedle

(a) He professed himself puzzled by Mrs Farland's illness. Was he? (Dr Parry saw little of her.)

(b) He was alone all Sunday afternoon.

(c) He seemed anxious to get rid of John.

(d) Nurse Ponting asked where his house was, and may have been on her way there.

(e) He was accustomed to offer tea, of the strong-flavoured sort, to patients, and did not drink this tea himself. If Nurse Ponting called, did he offer her a cup?

(f) If she did call, he did not mention the fact to John.

(g) He would have easy access to Sleepine.

V. Spiller, the Station-master

(a) Nurse Ponting showed interest in him and extracted the information that he was married.

(b) Of all the persons in the story, he had the least ready access to Sleepine—unless the drug was in Nurse Ponting's bag.

VI. Nurse Ponting

(a) Why did she come by the early train? Because she herself wanted to see someone in Creepe? Or because someone had told her to come by it? (Mr Walton? Dr Cheedle?) Or genuine error, due to 'thinking of the old 3.3'? If she came off her own bat, was it to see the station-master? Dr Cheedle? If somebody told her to come, was she a party to that arrangement? And if she was not, did her excursion into the town help or hinder the person who gave the instructions? Did either Dr Cheedle or John Farland know anything of her more than her name before her arrival? Did Dr Cheedle speak *directly* with her by 'phone or only hear from Dr Walton?

(*Note*: It might be expected that a nurse arriving at Creepe on a Sunday afternoon and finding herself with 3 hours to wait, would either (*a*) stay in the station or (*b*) visit either the doctor or one of the local hotels. Anybody going by way of the Square and Station Road would have a very good chance of meeting her, without going too obviously to the station. Her uniform would make her easy to recognise.)

(*b*) Apropos of this: Had she really been acquainted with the district and 'the old 3.3'? What were her antecedents? And did she know either the station-master or Dr Cheedle or the Farlands in earlier life? (She 'sharply' disclaimed all knowledge of 'five years ago'.)

(c) When she implied that there were drugs in her bag, did she mean the Sleepine? If so, did she bring it with her (for Mrs Farland)? Or get it from Dr Cheedle (for the same purpose)? And was she poisoned by her own drug? (the station-master?)

(d) Was the drug, on the other hand, obtained from some other source and the box slipped into her bag to create the impression that she had brought it?

Possible other sources:

Dr Cheedle's surgery (the doctor, his daughter, Dr Parry, John).

The cachets given to Millie by Dr Cheedle for Mrs Farland (Millie, John, Mr Walton), Farland's manufactory (John).

(e) How did Nurse Ponting get back to the station and when?

(a) The footstep on the bridge at 4.20?

(b) Some other time and route?

N.B. Here is where I must leave it to you to clear up approaches by way of goods yard, level-crossing, etc.

Note: that it is a dark, rainy winter afternoon, and that there are no trains, either on main line or branch, between 2.32 and 5.9, 'barring the goods', which was late and not cleared till 4.30. For possible times of arrival, see note on drug.

VII. P.C. Bratton

I have introduced this young man and his young woman with the idea that, if anybody wants to make John Farland the murderer, Bratton and Joan may supply the love-interest (since the murderer obviously can't have the love-interest). Joan at the hairdresser's might be a useful picker-up of gossip. No suspicion should, I think, be placed on Bratton, as he is too young to have any previous connection with Nurse Ponting (besides, he is a good character, since he helps an old woman with her parcels!).

Note on Sleepine. [Miss Sayers, with her customary accuracy of detail, used the name of an actual drug, but this has been altered to the fictitious 'Sleepine'.—Editor.] *(Collected in conversation with our local medical man.)*
Sleepine is one of the barbituric group, fairly new and much quicker and more powerful than veronal, medinal, luminal and the rest. It is on Part 1 of the Poisons Schedule, and is not available without a doctor's prescription.

The medicinal dose is 1½ grains; not more than 7½ gr. should be taken within 24 hours.

One big dose (10 gr. or over) would almost certainly be fatal to the ordinary person; still more certainly to anyone with an idiosyncrasy to the barbiturates.

It is a crystalline powder, usually supplied to physicians in cachets of 1½ gr., from which, of course, the powder could readily be extracted to drop into a cup or glass. It is freely soluble in water or alcohol and has an alkaline reaction to litmus. It has only a slight bitter taste, easily disguised in strong, sweet tea, whisky, cocktails, etc.

Effect: a large dose would take effect within half an hour, though this effect might be a little retarded if the patient moved about actively (walked to the station, for instance). It would produce deep sleep, passing into coma. In about two hours after administration the breathing would become stertorous (possibly passing later into breathing of Cheyne-Stokes type). The victim might not die for some hours after, but would in all probability never recover consciousness.

Treatment: Lumbar puncture and heroic doses of strychnine would be the only thing to try, but probably, with so large a dose, would do no good.

Poison Register: A doctor has to enter on his poison register only those poisons which he hands out to other people (nurses, patients' relatives, etc.) for administration. Poisons which he himself administers need not be so entered, and no track need be kept of them in his books or by his dispenser. Poisons are supposed to be kept under lock and key—'but they never are, you know!'

A Note on Creepe

Creepe is a small town of about 4,000 inhabitants, most of whom are employed about the works of Messrs Farland, manufacturing chemists. The station is only about a couple of minutes by car from the centre of the town.

The approach (Station Rd) and the entrance to the station are above the level of the line, so that passengers enter the station yard at the level of the two road bridges to east and west of the station and pass directly through the booking-hall on to the passenger bridge, from which lead (*a*) the stair to the Down platform, (*b*) the luggage lift, (*c*) the stair to the Up

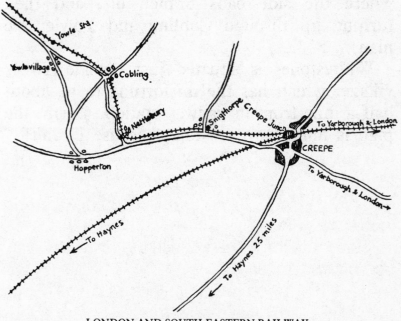

LONDON AND SOUTH-EASTERN RAILWAY
CREEPE AND PLUNTON BRANCH

platform and the Plunton Branch.

I think that on the far side of the branch, the ground stretches away level—i.e., no cutting on this side—so that there would be streets, etc., on the lower level, with a gate or some such thing leading to the station precincts. I imagine that the goods yards and siding would be somewhere round about here, but have not ventured to embark on this.

The quickest way to Yowle and Plunton by road is by the side-road through Nettlebury and Cobling, the line taken by the railway. The omnibus, however, goes round so as to take in the hamlet of Hopperton, dropping passengers for Snigthorpe and Nettlebury at the points where the side-roads branch off, and then turning up through Cobling and Yowle (see plan).

Whitestones is situated just outside Yowle village, which has the misfortune to be about half a mile from its railway station. (Mem. the plan is not drawn to scale, because I can't!)

PART TWO

by Freeman Wills Crofts

I

Inspector James Billingham of the Eastshire County Constabulary enjoyed the approval of his superiors, the loyal attachment of his men, and the respect of the public: some considerable achievement when you come to think of it. From these facts it will be deduced that he was good at his job, unassuming in his manner, and kindly to those beneath him in the service.

He was second in command in that diminutive department which the Chief Constable of Eastshire was wont to refer to as 'my C.I.D.' That is to say that in the Yarborough area of the County he was invariably detailed to investigate occurrences which had an appearance of mystery or which looked like serious crimes.

Creepe was in the Yarborough area, and so it happened that when Sergeant Craven of the Creepe station telephoned that he wanted assistance in what looked like a poisoning case, it was Billingham who was sent.

The summons reached the Inspector at an unfortunate moment. He had just reached home

37

and was sitting down to supper when the telephone rang. Billingham was tired and hungry, and sighed as he hung up the receiver.

'What is it?' asked his wife.

'Wanted at Creepe,' he explained. 'Some woman found dead.'

'They can just wait,' declared Mrs Billingham with profound contempt for 'them'. 'Not one step shall you go till you've had your supper.'

The Inspector had a very proper respect for his Chief's authority, but he had more for his wife's, particularly when, as in this instance, her fiat was in accordance with his own desires. 'Ten minutes won't hurt,' he therefore conceded, and sitting down, he made an intensive use of the time.

Fortified for what might be coming, Billingham reached headquarters in due course. There concise instructions were awaiting him. He was to take the small Ford, drive to Creepe, and assist in whatever was required.

Sergeant Craven was a big burly man with a round good-humoured face and a passion for making jokes which delighted himself, if no one else. But when a little later Billingham walked into his office, the sergeant was not smiling. Instead he looked worried.

'Glad you've come over, sir,' he greeted his visitor. 'We've got a case of what looks like suicide, but Dr Cheedle's a bit mysterious about it, throwing out hints and so on.'

38

'What does he say?' Billingham asked shortly. The instalment method of narration always irritated him.

'He says it looks a bit puzzling to him, and for me to go into it thoroughly and not to take anything for granted.'

This made no greater appeal to Billingham. 'Well, you'd have done that in any case, wouldn't you?' he retorted.

'Yes, sir, of course. But I thought he was suggesting it might be murder.'

'Get on and let's have the facts,' Billingham snorted.

'It was Constable Bratton, sir, rang up. He's off duty this evening and he went to the station to meet his young lady. When he was there, just about 5.20, they found this woman,' and Craven went on to tell of the discovery of Nurse Ponting's body in the ladies' cloakroom. 'I got Dr Cheedle and the ambulance and we took her to the Cottage Hospital, but she died about half an hour ago.'

'Did she regain consciousness?'

'No, sir.' Craven paused, then went on: 'I've got preliminary statements from the people concerned. It seems she called on Dr Cheedle this afternoon. He says she was perfectly normal at that time, and that's why he doesn't think suicide's likely.'

Billingham read the statements. As far as he

could make out from them, the deceased woman was a Nurse Ponting, on her way from London to take charge of a patient at Yowle. She had arrived at Creepe at 2.32, apparently expecting to find a connection to Yowle. There being none till five, she had called on Dr Cheedle, who was attending her prospective patient and who had presumably sent for her. They had discussed the case for some fifteen minutes and then the nurse had left, seeming perfectly normal in every way. That was at a minute or two before three. So far as was known, she had not been seen from that time until she was discovered unconscious at the station.

'That all you've done?' went on the Inspector.

'I'm afraid that's all, sir,' Craven answered with a worried expression. 'There hasn't been much time, what with getting the woman to the hospital and all.'

Billingham nodded. 'I'm not complaining: I only want to know where I am. We had better go along and see this doctor. Ring up, will you, and find out if he's got home.'

Ten minutes later the two police officers were seated in Cheedle's consulting-room.

'I've seen your statement to Craven, sir,' Billingham explained, 'but it was necessarily hurried, and I'd be obliged if you could give me some further details. What about the woman herself to start with? You engaged her, I presume?'

'As a matter of fact, I didn't,' the doctor returned, 'though she was engaged with my full approval. What happened was this: A nurse was wanted for my patient, Mrs Farland, of Yowle, and owing to the influenza epidemic I couldn't get one locally. Mr Walton, who is solicitor to Mrs Farland, and whom I met there, mentioned that he thought his doctor son, who is in Harley Street, might be able to get one. I asked him to try and he sent Nurse Ponting.'

'Then you know nothing of her personally?'

'Nothing except what I saw this afternoon. She seemed an ordinary competent woman, in normal good spirits, and was looking forward to being with her patient by six o'clock.' Dr Cheedle paused and looked curiously at Billingham. 'That was all I saw for myself, but she told me something which interested me quite a lot.'

'And that was, sir?'

'Do you remember the Heaviside murder case?'

'Not the Carlisle case of three years ago?'

'Yes.'

'I remember it well. I read every word of it. It's in the Famous Trials series.'

'I thought so. I'd forgotten the details myself,

41

but the nurse reminded me of them. Heaviside poisoned his wife.'

'Yes, sir. The doctor missed it;' there was the faintest suspicion of a smile in Billingham's eyes; 'but the nurse caught it on. It was her evidence hanged Heaviside.'

Cheedle nodded shortly. 'This is the nurse,' he declared.

Billingham whistled. 'You don't say so!' he exclaimed. 'That's a bit suggestive certainly.' He paused, then resumed: 'I understand she died of poison. Is that so?'

'In her bag was found a small box labelled "Sleepine" and containing a single cachet which looked like Sleepine. She had all the symptoms of an overdose of Sleepine and no others. It therefore looks as if she had died from the drug, but without a post-mortem I can't say so with certainty.'

'Sleepine? A sleeping draught, isn't it?'

Cheedle's manner became slightly professorial. 'Sleepine is one of the barbituric group, fairly new and more powerful than veronal, medinal, luminal and the rest. From one to two grains makes a useful opiate, but a large dose, say ten grains or more, would normally prove fatal.'

'It's on Part I of the Poisons Schedule, I think?'

'Yes, it cannot be purchased without a doctor's prescription.'

42

'But a nurse could get it without?'

Cheedle shrugged. Billingham took silence for consent and turned to another point.

'She left you about three this afternoon, Craven says?'

'Just before three. I heard the Market clock strike just after I had returned to my room from letting her out.'

'Did you think she was in a frame of mind which might have led her to suicide?'

'I certainly did not. She was in good spirits and interested in the case at Yowle to which she was going. No, I saw absolutely nothing to suggest suicide: quite the contrary.'

'And I suppose an accident of that sort in the case of a nurse is out of the question?'

'None of us is immune from error,' Cheedle pointed out with a suspicious twinkle in his eye, 'but I admit she seemed to have her head well screwed on.'

Billingham rubbed his chin, a characteristic action when thinking deeply. 'It looks badly enough,' he declared presently. 'Tell me, doctor, has this stuff much of a taste?'

'Not much. Slightly bitter.'

'Could it be easily disguised?'

'Yes, I think so. Strong sweet tea, whisky, cocktails and so on. One might notice something about the taste, but not enough, I think, to make one suspicious.'

'Quite.' Billingham sat again in thought.

43

'Another point,' he went on. 'From the state she was in at 5.25 and the time of her death, which I understand was just on eight o'clock, are you in a position to say when she took the dose?'

Dr Cheedle hesitated. 'Assuming that she did take Sleepine, which we don't know for certain yet, I should say that she must have had it about two hours before I saw her at the station: say about half-past three: very approximately, of course. It might have been earlier or later.'

'About half an hour after she left you. That would just give her time to find a teashop or,' Billingham hesitated in his turn, 'for someone to offer her a drink. Well then, what would happen? How soon would the stuff take effect? When would she begin to feel sleepy?'

'Impossible to say with any degree of exactitude, because as you probably know, different people have a different tolerance to these drugs.'

'I understand that, doctor,' Billingham agreed, a trifle impatient with this manifestation of the scientific attitude; 'but assuming an average tolerance?'

'I should expect a large dose to take effect in about half an hour.'

'About four o'clock. And what would the effect be?'

'Sleepiness, deep sleep, coma, death.'

'Speaking approximately, would it be correct
44

to say that if the nurse reached the waiting-room before about four she could have walked, but if after four, she must have been carried?'

Cheedle was unwilling to commit himself, but at last, subject to modification by facts which might subsequently come to light, he agreed that the Inspector's estimate was reasonable. Billingham then turned to the subject of the certificate. 'Can you give one from what you have seen?'

Here the doctor was emphatic. He certainly could give no certificate without a post-mortem. Hadn't he told the Inspector that all that he had been saying was tentative, and dependent on Sleepine in large quantity being found in the remains?

'Then I'll see the coroner and fix it up.' Billingham rose. 'Thank you very much, doctor. Sorry to have been such a nuisance.'

'It's suspicious enough,' he went on as he and Craven walked back towards the police station. 'Here's this nurse, mixed up with a poison case and murder trial at which she made a good many enemies, and she dies under circumstances which suggest murder. Very suspicious, I will say.'

'That's so, sir. Still, after three years do you think—'

'I was guessing, of course. We may find she has vamped some other woman's best boy. Now

45

see here, Craven: first thing in the morning you start in to trace her movements after she left the doctor. Find out if she had a drink anywhere or if anyone saw her. Have you enough men for it?'

'Yes, sir, I'll manage.'

'And you'd better go now and see the coroner and fix up about the post-mortem and the inquest. While you're doing that I'll have a word with this solicitor, Walton, and try to pick up something about the nurse. Where does he live?'

'"Parkley", Priory Avenue.' Craven pointed. 'First turn to the left down London Road.'

II

Inspector Billingham was in greater luck than he could have hoped for. When he reached 'Parkley' not only was Mr Walton, the solicitor, at home, but he had staying with him for the week-end his Harley Street son. And it was because of this fact that Billingham obtained a piece of information which otherwise he might have missed.

He decided to take the possibility of the nurse's suicide first. 'You knew her, doctor,' he said. 'Can you suggest any reason why she should have been dissatisfied with life?'

Young Walton shook his head. 'Certainly not

to the extent of suicide. I could see that at first she was very unwilling to go to Yowle, but in the end she clearly decided it would be best for her to take the job.'

Billingham was slightly puzzled. 'I don't quite follow that. Why should she be unwilling to take the job?'

'No reason whatever,' the elder Walton interrupted shortly.

His son looked at him curiously. 'Oh, well, I think we should tell the Inspector why she was chosen, you know, Dad.'

'There's nothing to tell.'

'There must be, sir, after that,' Billingham said with a smile. 'I hope you will tell me.'

'It's very improper,' the lawyer retorted. 'You shouldn't have said anything about it, Charles.'

'I'm not so sure. I always think it's better to explain everything to the police. After all, the Inspector's not a fool. He'll understand the position.'

'You've no right to make unfounded insinuations against those Yowle people,' declared Walton Senior. 'I wash my hands of the whole thing.'

Billingham, now thoroughly interested, had another shot. 'I'd be grateful for your ideas, sir, all the same. You know nothing will be used improperly against anyone.'

The lawyer shrugged. 'The mischief's done,'

he complained; 'we shall have to tell you. But I protest, and I remind you that my private ideas are not proof and cannot be used for any purpose whatever. This is a piece of pure guesswork and should never have been mentioned.'

'I'll remember that, sir.'

'Well, if you must know,' the old man went on in an aggrieved way, 'I am solicitor to a Mrs Farland of Yowle. She's been ill for some time and Dr Cheedle has been attending her. The illness was—well,' he made a gesture of annoyance, 'I shouldn't say it, but it was rather mysterious. I could see Dr Cheedle wasn't satisfied; in fact he spoke of a consultation. Well, I'm her solicitor, as I said.' He paused. 'I spoke to him about a nurse and he said he could not get one locally owing to this epidemic of 'flu. It occurred to me that this gave an opportunity of getting a highly trained nurse from Town, and I asked the doctor if he would care for me to arrange it through my son. He said he would be pleased. So I asked my son and—he sent Nurse Ponting.'

'Yes,' went on the son, 'and I might just add the part that you've left out. My father wasn't satisfied that all was right, and told me so. I knew Nurse Ponting had nursed in a poisoning case. I told her straight what was in our minds. I said we wanted her to say nothing, but simply to keep her eyes open. If she saw anything she

48

thought suspicious, she was to consult Dr Cheedle. The reason she wasn't anxious to go was that she was afraid of running into another poisoning case. Natural enough, too. But she didn't want to refuse a good job.'

'You see now why I objected to saying anything, Inspector?' the old man put in. 'Such a suggestion carries with it a tacit accusation of murder against someone. Neither my son nor I has the slightest right to make any such suggestion, and neither of us does make it.'

'I understand that very well, sir. But I'm obliged for what I'll consider as an anonymous hint.'

Though Billingham spoke lightly, he was considerably impressed by what he had heard. Lawyer Walton was reputed to be a shrewd man, and if he had become suspicious of Mrs Farland's illness it showed there really was something to suspect. And Cheedle was an old ninny. What had happened was as clear as daylight. Walton thought that Mrs Farland was being poisoned and that Cheedle was not alive to it. He had seen a chance of finding out and he had taken it. And now the nurse, going down with this special knowledge, had died suddenly before seeing her patient. Huh! The case was getting more involved. Billingham considered for a moment, then asked in as natural a tone as he could: 'Is she as well to do as she is reputed to be, this Mrs Farland?'

Walton glared at his son. 'As her solicitor, I'm not bound to answer that,' he said wrathfully.

'Of course not, sir,' the Inspector admitted. He did not want to antagonise the lawyer and thought discretion was indicated. If he really required the information he could always get powers to obtain it. He rose. 'Then if you don't feel like going into that, I'll be getting along. I'm greatly obliged for your hint, which I'll keep strictly to myself.'

As he left the lawyer's, Billingham glanced at his watch. Ten o'clock: too late to do anything more that night. After a call at the police station he turned the Ford's bonnet homewards. From the Yarborough station he made a telephonic report to his Chief Constable and called it a day.

While there was as yet no conclusive evidence, it seemed increasingly likely to Billingham that the case would prove one of murder. It looked indeed as if this might be the great chance for which he had been so long hoping, and which up to now had eluded him. If it turned out to be murder, and if he handled it well, it could scarcely fail to mean advancement. How he hoped he would be given a free hand with the investigation! Fortunately the Chief was not fond of outside help. He would undoubtedly prefer to keep at home any kudos that was going. What Billingham was afraid of was the Yard, but he believed that if he could show reasonable progress, he would be allowed to continue unaided.

He was thankful to be in no doubt as to his procedure. All sorts of inquiries were crying out to be made and for a day or two at least his work was cut out for him.

None of the railway staff, he imagined, was likely to be involved: at least inquiry in that quarter might be postponed. What was more important was to get more detailed statements from those two persons, John Farland and Millie Pink, both of whom Sergeant Craven's notes showed were connected with Mrs Farland of the mysterious illness, and both of whom had been present when the nurse was found.

III

John Farland had been described as assistant manager of the Chemical Works, and thither next morning Billingham and Craven directed their steps. Youthful though Farland was, it was evident from the manner of the clerk who took their names that he was a person of some importance in the establishment. He saw them immediately. He had a pleasant rather offhand manner, but beneath it Billingham felt he could detect strain, as if the affair had given the man a shock.

'The statement you made to the sergeant last

night, Mr Farland, was necessarily brief,' Billingham began, 'and we've come round to get something a bit more detailed. I should be obliged if you'd tell everything you can, no matter how trivial the incidents may seem.'

'I'll do my best,' the young man returned. 'Just what do you want to know?'

'Better cover everything and be done with it. Tell me all you did and saw, say, from lunch till dinner on Sunday.'

'As you like. If I don't make myself clear you can ask questions.'

'You need have no fear,' Billingham assured him. Farland smiled painfully and began.

His statement however proved disappointing. It threw no light on the affair, about which indeed he seemed himself completely puzzled. He described his lunch at Mrs Farland's and his conversation with Millie Pink about going to the *Hymn of Praise*. He had, he said, driven her to the church, arriving about half-past two, the hour at which the service was to begin. Then he had driven to Dr Cheedle's, and had been disappointed to find that Miss Cheedle, whom he had been hoping to take for a drive, was not at home. The doctor didn't invite him in then, but asked him to go back later for tea. He subsequently felt rather at a loose end. First he thought of driving over to see some friends at Yarborough, but it seemed not worth while because of the weather, so he went to his rooms instead. He sat there and read till about quarter to five, when he returned to Dr Cheedle's. He had expected to pick up Miss Pink there, but as she didn't call, he decided to go to the station and drive both her and the nurse to Mrs Farland's. He went to the station, and it was when he was there that the nurse was found. Miss Pink had actually made the discovery and it had upset her a good deal. He had eventually driven her to her aunt's, where he had dined, returning to Creepe later in the evening.

It was one of Inspector Billingham's precepts that the truth of every statement made to him in the course of an investigation must be doubted until checked. Though he had no reason to question this of John Farland's, routine demanded that any available corroboration should be obtained. He therefore rang up Dr Cheedle, and asked him if he had seen John on the previous day, and if so, what had taken place at the interviews.

The doctor promptly confirmed what John had said, and Billingham went on to interview Mrs Humphries, the young man's landlady. Her corroboration was equally emphatic. Mr Farland had gone out about twelve—he had lunched out. Shortly before three he had come in, told her that he would be going out to tea, and settled down in his sitting-room, which was next to the kitchen where she herself was sitting. About half-past four she had heard him go upstairs to his bedroom, and then a few minutes later he had gone out. She had expected him for dinner, but he had dined out, not turning up till after ten.

Knowing how to do such things without arousing suspicion, Billingham got the somewhat garrulous landlady to let him see John Farland's rooms, and a significant fact struck him immediately.

That was that the window of Farland's ground-floor sitting-room opened on to a yard, from which it would be easy to get into the street without much risk of being seen from the kitchen. Therefore the young man's alibi was by no means watertight.

Millie Pink's name was the next on the list. To save time, Billingham checked a point in her preliminary statement by telephoning to the sexton of St Sebastian's Church, where the *Hymn of Praise* had been given. This confirmed her assertion that she had been to the church on Sunday afternoon. She hadn't looked well, the sexton said, and had asked for a seat near the door, saying she had a headache which might grow too bad to let her sit the service out. He had kept his eye on her, being afraid she might faint, and had seen her leave before the service was over.

So Millie's alibi wasn't watertight either, Billingham reflected, and after lunch both he and Craven went down to see her at Yowle. As

54

they approached the Whitestones door Dr Cheedle came out. He beckoned Billingham over.

'You got my note?' he asked.

The Inspector shook his head.

'You must have left before it arrived,' Cheedle went on. 'I sent it just before lunch. It's about that post-mortem. There were over twelve grains of Sleepine in Nurse Ponting's body.'

'Just what you thought, sir,' Billingham said diplomatically. 'Well, that's that. A fatal dose, and not likely to result from accident or suicide. There were no other indications? No signs of violence or anything of that kind?'

'None.'

'We've come down to get Miss Pink's account of the finding of the nurse. She's Miss Farland's niece, is she not?'

'Yes.'

Billingham grew confidential. 'Some money about here by the look of things,' he considered. 'The old lady must surely be well-to-do.'

But Dr Cheedle was not to be drawn. His manner stiffened. 'I really don't know anything of her finances,' he declared shortly, and with a nod drove off.

Millie kept them waiting for several minutes, coming down at last dishevelled and apologetic. She was clearly still upset from her experiences, though she was willing enough to talk about them. Her statement was confused, and Billingham had to ask a good many questions before he could get it straight in his mind.

She had had, Millie said, a nasty headache all that Sunday, and that had made her even more doubtful about going to the musical service than she would otherwise have been. However, she thought she would risk it. But during the service her headache had got much worse, and she had given up an idea she had had of going for tea to the vicarage. Nevertheless, she had left the church before the service was over, but only to walk in the air with the hope of relieving her aching head. Instead of getting better, however, it had got worse, and when she found herself near the station, she had gone into the waiting-room to rest and dry her clothes, for it had been raining and she was wet. In the waiting-room she had fallen asleep, but had been roused by the arrival of the Branch train at five o'clock. She had been going to take her place in it, but she had seen a young man on the platform whom she didn't wish to meet—Mr Holford, the estate agent's son, if the Inspector must know, who had recently been more friendly than she quite cared about—so she remained where she was. The two main-line trains passed and for the second time she had been about to take her seat, when she had heard a strange sound of heavy breathing. She had run out and called to the men on the platform. They had looked in the cloakroom and discovered the nurse. She had had a great shock and was much upset. She had of course missed her train, but fortunately for her Mr John Farland had come to meet the nurse, and he had driven her home.

'Now that I'm here,' said Billingham, when she had concluded, 'I'd like a word with Mrs Farland if she's well enough to see me.'

'Oh, yes, Inspector!' Millie exclaimed. 'She'll love to see you. I'm sure she'd be very angry with me if I let you leave the house without seeing her.'

She went off to tell her aunt that he was there, and Billingham sat wondering. He was beginning to think that he was up against something more difficult and complicated than he had anticipated. The inquiry had only just begun, but already he had discovered two people who might have given the Sleepine to Nurse Ponting at half-past three on Sunday afternoon—John Farland and Millie Pink. Neither of them could produce a witness to show where they had been at that hour. Millie's story that she was vaguely wandering in the rain might be true. So might John Farland's that he was reading in his sitting-room. On the other hand, either of them might be false.

But how, the Inspector asked himself, could Millie or John—each of them strangers to

Nurse Ponting-have induced her to take twelve grains of Sleepine, no matter how innocently it might have been disguised?

A giggling, hare-brained flapper might accept refreshment from a stranger in a strange town. They often did—hence the White Slave traffic. But Nurse Ponting had been an experienced, middle-aged woman, familiar with drugs and poisons, and probably well acquainted with the seamy side of life, as most nurses are.

Opportunity, therefore, was the only reason up to now for suspecting either Millie or John. So far, said Billingham to himself, it was certainly a hell of a case.

He heard Millie's loose shoes clattering down the stairs, and he got up to meet her at the door. In her usual breathless way she led him to an upper floor and ushered him into her aunt's bedroom.

Billingham, in common with most other people of the neighbourhood, had heard rumours about the sort of woman Mrs Farland was. Nevertheless he was a little taken aback when he entered the over-heated, over-perfumed and over-furnished room in which she was lying in bed.

Evidently she had stage-managed her reception of him. Her lace-topped nightdress was carefully arranged to display a glimpse of bare white shoulder, her scarlet-tipped hands were sparkling with rings, and she was lying at the extreme edge of the bed in order that a watery ray of sunlight, shining in through the window, should fall on her waved and henna'd hair.

She let her eyelids droop coyly, then lifted them languorously again to stare at him in a way which he could only describe as 'ogling'.

'I am so happy to see you, Inspector,' she cooed at him, and stretched out her hand in a way which made him think that she intended him to kiss it.

He got out of that, however, because she suddenly noticed that Millie was still standing in the doorway, and snapped at her to leave them alone.

Millie shut the door and clattered away, and the Inspector sat down on the chair which had been placed ready for him by the bedside. Feeling rather uneasy in face of Mrs Farland's fluttering eyelids and toothy smile, he plunged into business immediately.

'I really have no right to disturb you, Mrs Farland, and of course you needn't tell me anything unless you wish to...'

'But I do,' she broke in.

The cooing note had gone out of her voice; she spoke in a whisper. Forgetting the ray of sunlight, she leant towards him. Her rouged face was suddenly haggard and tense.

'I am being poisoned, Inspector!' she whispered.

Billingham was a hard-boiled police officer, but it gave him an odd thrill of horror to hear her say that. She was so helpless, so stupidly vain, and so dreadfully afraid.

'What makes you think that?' he asked.

'Isn't that obvious? I was a young, active woman till a few months ago. Then why am I so ill now? There is no reason for me to be ill.'

That was an absurd argument, he thought. Perhaps the early medical opinion, that she was merely hysterical, would turn out to be the right one after all.

'Whom do you suppose is poisoning you?' he asked.

'John Farland—Millie Pink—Penelope Cheedle. It might be any of them—they are all waiting for me to die. I keep changing my will, Inspector,' she whispered, 'hoping that whoever is trying to kill me will give up when they know they won't get anything if I die. But I don't get any better.'

'So you definitely suspect one of those three?'

She shook her head, her lips trembling.

'No, no. I don't want to. I don't want to suspect anybody. But I know it can't be the servants—they've no reason to want me to die. Besides, I've changed them all two or three times since I began suspecting things. And then that nurse...'

'What about the nurse?' Billingham interrupted. 'Did you know her?'

'No.' She moistened her bright red lips. 'But I know about her now. I've read all the papers. She was a nurse who understood poisons. Walton and Cheedle between them brought her here to save my life. They haven't said so, but I know they did. And whoever is trying to kill me, killed her first.'

Her frightened eyes stared into his, and he felt that odd thrill of horror go through him again.

'Don't you see?' she said huskily. 'If the nurse were here it would be so much more difficult. It's awful to accuse one's friends, but there's Penelope Cheedle, too. She wants to marry John, but I know they don't feel like doing it on his small income. Oh, it's terrible, Inspector—it's terrible!'

She began to weep. He tried clumsily to soothe her. She took one of his big hands and held it tightly, while she lay back on the pillow, with her tears making furrows in the thick rouge on her cheeks.

'Don't let them kill me, Inspector,' she sobbed. 'I—I don't want to die.'

'You'll be all right,' he said gruffly. 'Perhaps I'd better get Miss Pink now.'

He got up rather hurriedly and left the room, feeling embarrassed. It was a daft household, he thought. Ten to one hysteria was at the back of it all ... Yet somebody had undoubtedly murdered Nurse Ponting.

61

Suddenly a thought struck him. What had Penelope Cheedle been doing on Sunday afternoon? He knew her well by sight and had always admired her. Surely a girl like that, a pure, sweet, lovely girl, couldn't have committed cold-blooded murder? But why not?

He was so absorbed by his thoughts that he forgot to look for Millie Pink, and left the house without seeing anybody.

Upstairs in the over-scented, over-heated, over-furnished bedroom Mrs Farland heard him start his car and drive away.

A whimper of terror left her painted lips. She clenched her hands over her heart, and her frightened eyes sent quick, darting glances into all corners of the room.

It was a cold, dull day. The heat of the room had made the windows misty, and the light that came in seemed grey and somehow dead. It made strange watery shadows and queer reflections on the polished furniture.

She lay stretched out in the bed, tense and horribly cold. Only her eyes moved, and she seemed scarcely to breathe.

'He's gone!' she thought. 'He didn't believe me. They'll do it now. They won't dare to wait much longer.'

There was a thud on the windowpane, a scrabbling of claws. She leapt up in bed with a scream.

It was only a young blackbird, frightened and

62

mystified by the glass, but as she stared at its dark fluttering wings, hysteria welled up inside her, and she screamed for Millie at the top of her voice.

It was the Angel of Death, her poor, panic-stricken brain insisted, the Angel of Death, trying to break into her room!

NOTES

Map of Town and Station at Creepe Municipal Car Park
Full up in summer, but on wet winter's afternoon empty. No attendant. Not overlooked. Back fenced with plain wire fence, from which it is easy to trespass to Batt's Lane. This not overlooked, except by chance of a passer-by on Batt's Lane.

Lynn Road
Deserted on a wet Sunday afternoon in winter. Not overlooked. Watchman at Chemical Works would be in his hut at back of buildings. After the goods has passed the station staff would clear away to shelter. No houses along Lynn Road. Car could be parked outside railway gates unseen. A metalled cartroad from Goods Yard gate to Point A. From Point A a well-trodden path to platforms.

John Farland's Rooms

Kept by a widow, Mrs Humphries. She has no family and there are only the two in the house. She sits in the kitchen, which looks out at side of house towards station. John's sitting-room is on ground floor on side next Priory Avenue, his bedroom over it.

It seemed to me from Miss Sayers' instalment that only Cheedle could be guilty. Therefore I thought he might be left for the readers' choice and I sketched out the outline of a scheme for John Farland's guilt. This can be accepted or rejected as desired. It is obviously not complete, and some good reason (police regulations?) for John leaving his car in the park and not outside his house should be thought out.

I am assuming that the following happened. Obviously it need not be assumed by anybody else.

What Really Happened

Solicitor Walton

Walton suspected poisoning and thought Cheedle, while perfectly honest, was muffing things.

He therefore suggested the nurse, mentioning 'mental' as a blind, but really asking his son to send a nurse who was an authority on poisons.

Walton, M.D., chose a nurse who had been the chief witness in a poisoning case in Carlisle.

It was a murder case and her evidence secured the conviction of the accused. This case had been published in the Famous Trials series, with a photograph of the nurse. Nurse Ponting had had to leave Carlisle in order to get another job. Her history was known to Walton, M.D.

He sees her before starting and tells her what she has to look out for.

Nurse Ponting
Is worried by job, but she daren't antagonise Walton by refusing it. She decides to see Cheedle beforehand and comes by an earlier train in order to give her the excuse of doing so. She pretends surprise at station that there is no Yowle connection, as she does not want this to become known.

She calls on Cheedle, who tells her straight he fears poison. They talk about the precautions she is to observe. She leaves, intending to get some tea, as Cheedle has not offered her any.

Time-table: 2.30 Reaches Creepe Station.
2.40 Reaches Cheedle's.
2.55 Leaves Cheedle's.

John Farland
Is the murderer of Mrs Farland. At the works he has prepared a bottle of pills similar to heart pills taken by Mrs Farland, but putting a varying amount of arsenic into each. Pills he has

placed at the bottom of bottle have a large quantity. The cumulative effect of the bottle will be to kill. (Or several bottles). He has managed to change his bottle for Mrs Farland's when she was asleep, and unknown to all in the house.

Being interested in the subject he has read carefully all books on poisoning and poison trials.

1.45 *Sunday:* John has conversation with Millie at Mrs Farland's.

2.30 *Sunday:* Having driven Millie to Creepe, leaves her at church.

2.38 *Sunday:* Having called on Cheedle, leaves him. John's car is parked at Cheedle's door.

2.39 *Sunday:* As John is starting up car the nurse goes up to Cheedle's door. John recognises her as Nurse Ponting of the Carlisle case, having seen her photograph in one of his books. He drives off, completely upset. This means that Walton was suspicious.

John sees that his game is up. Either they will find who is trying to poison Mrs Farland, or at least they will save her life, and he will lose the £15,000 he wants to marry Cheedle's daughter.

He drives his car into the park to think. In a moment of insane panic, he decides he must murder the nurse. Then he will somehow arrange for an increased dose of arsenic to be given Mrs Farland, before anyone else can be got.

He has a bottle of Sleepine which he always carries and which he got from the works, so that he can commit suicide if the attempt to murder Mrs Farland is discovered. A plan occurs to him.

2.42 *Sunday:* He leaves his car in the park, walks to his rooms and enters noisily. He calls to his landlady that he will be staying in for some time, but going out for tea. He apparently settles down in his room. He puts in a bag a couple of bottles of Indian tonic, glasses and a box of biscuits, slips silently out of his window, hurries across the waste ground to his car, puts the bag on board, goes back to Market Square and watches Cheedle's house.

2.56 *Sunday:* He sees the nurse leave, introduces himself, says he is going to his aunt's, and asks may he drive her down. She is pleased and agrees. She says she wants to call at station for her bag. He says, Certainly, but he wants just to make a short call in the suburbs first. He leads to car park. They are unseen.

3.05 *Sunday:* They leave park and he drives out six miles into a deserted wood. There he switches off engine, saying it has failed, gets out, and lest the nurse should know about cars, disconnects ignition. He says he can get

67

tea and a tow a little further on. He asks her to wait and walks out of sight. After a time he returns to say he can get no tea, but a tow will be coming shortly. By a lucky chance he has some tonic and biscuits from a previous trip—will she join him in cold comfort?

3.30 *Sunday:* She doesn't want any, but he persuades her. He puts a dose of Sleepine into the tonic. She drinks it. Then fumbling with the engine, he reconnects. He says he can get them back to Creepe, though not as far as Yowle. They start back (3.45).

3.55 *Sunday:* He approaches Creepe by Lynn Road and stops at goods-yard gate. The car is unseen. The nurse is now getting sleepy, and when he tells her there is a good fire in the waiting-room, and that this is a short way there, she lets him help her out. They walk down cartroad and past A to Up Platform. She gets sleepier.

4.15 *Sunday:* He is afraid to leave her in the waiting-room, so opens lavatory and carries her in. He puts box of Sleepine in her bag, gets quickly back to car, drives back to park, climbs fence and slips silently into his sitting-room through window. He makes a noise, goes loudly upstairs, calls a remark to his landlady, walks out, regains car and reaches Cheedle's, as in Miss Sayers' chapter.

4.45 *Sunday:* After the discovery of the nurse's body he drives Millie home. There, seeing his attempt to murder Mrs Farland will be frustrated if delayed, he somehow contrives to leave a dose of poison which will be given to Mrs Farland on the following day.

Note: If the question of goods-yard gate being open on Sunday afternoon arises, this difficulty might be met

(*a*) Either by a special arrangement whereby some farmer delivered perishable traffic on

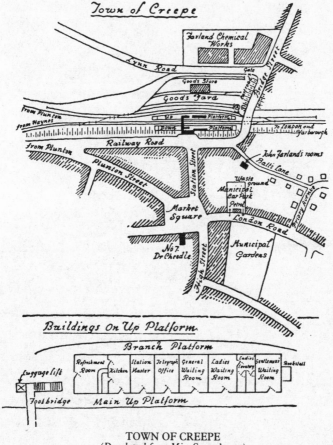

TOWN OF CREEPE
(*Developed from Miss Sayers' map*)

Sunday afternoon, which John knew of, the porter not locking the gate till he was going off duty, or

(*b*) That in his capacity of assistant manager of the Works, John should have a key. Neither of these very good, I'm afraid.

PART THREE

by *Valentine Williams*

I

On Monday evening, the evening following the
Creepe Station tragedy, Penelope Cheedle dined
at Whitestones, Mrs Farland's house.

John Farland would have taken her there,
but he had previously arranged to attend a
Works' smoking concert at Creepe, so he
compromised by lending her his Austin,
declaring confidently that he would find
someone to give him a lift out to Yowle, and
would arrive at Whitestones early enough to
drive her home to the doctor's house.

In Mrs Farland's sombre dining-room, with
the late Mr Farland's golf-cups gleaming on the
fumed oak sideboard, Penelope shared a fried
sole and mutton hash with Millie Pink, waited
on by Agnes, the elderly housemaid, for it was
the parlourmaid's night out.

They had reached the dessert when Nurse
Cran, dressed for the street, popped her head
in.

'I'm off,' she announced. 'She seems much
better tonight. I've filled the hot-water bottle
and that blessed Peke of hers has had his

71

dinner. You've only to warm up her Benger's on the gas ring at 10, one of you, and give her her cachet and she'll be as right as right. By the way,' she went on, 'there's only one cachet left. Your Pa, Miss Cheedle, promised to send along another bottle. I think you should ring him up and remind him.'

'My father's over at Cobling at a confinement,' explained Penelope. 'He said he'd probably be home late.'

'Then maybe Dr Parry could run out with a bottle from the dispensary. Or perhaps the chemist would oblige: he ought to have a prescription, really, but he's supplied it to us before—Sleepine, you know. And that reminds me—anything fresh about poor Nurse Ponting?'

'Not as far as I know,' said Millie, 'except the Inquest's tomorrow and I shall have to give evidence. Dear me, I feel so scared.'

'Mrs Farland seems ever so excited about it this evening, her picture in the paper an' all,' Nurse Cran confided. 'I really believe it's done the poor thing good. I suppose it's taken her back to the old days when she was always having her picture in the papers. It's an ill wind, as they say! Well, good night, all!' At the door she turned back. 'By the way, she wants the evening paper, d'reckly it comes. That's her ringing for it now!'

While a bell whirred imperiously from the

floor above, Millie Pink, with a guilty air, produced the newspaper, upon which she had been sitting, and fled.

Left alone, Penelope finished her apple and lit a cigarette. Presently, the window was tapped from outside. She ran to it, parted the curtains. The window was open at the top.

'Who is it?' she cried.

It was misty in the garden. A tall form loomed among the evergreens.

'It's me, Parry!' a muffled voice replied. 'I've brought Mrs Farland's cachets.'

'Wait! I'll let you in,' the girl said.

She led Dr Parry into the dining-room.

'I didn't want to ring,' he explained, lowering his voice. 'If she discovered that I'd set foot in the house, whew! The last time I was here she flew into a proper paddy simply because I said . . .'

Penelope laughed. 'That a little taste of Stalin wouldn't hurt a lot of people in this country! I know. She still goes on about it.'

'She told your father that I'm nothing but a dangerous Bolshevik!'

'Well, so you are, aren't you, David?'

Through his horn-rimmed spectacles, he surveyed her. He made two of her, a strapping young man, in his cycling overalls, dark-haired and resolute-looking with a somewhat sardonic expression.

'I'm not a bloated industrialist like John

Farland,' he remarked, not unhumorously.

'Bloated industrialist! Why, you know he's scarcely got enough to live on.'

'Oh, well, don't let's talk about him. I love you in blue, Penny.'

She dropped him a little bob.

'I never seem to see you alone any more,' he grumbled with an injured air.

She sighed. 'You're not going to start that all over again, David?'

He shrugged his broad shoulders. 'Okay! Here's the Sleepine for dear Aunt Emma. Your father left me a note before he started for Cobling, asking me to deliver it without fail tonight.'

'She's down to the last cachet in the old bottle, it seems.'

By mutual consent they moved out into the hall. She accompanied him as far as the garden gate. A motor-cycle was propped there, smelling of hot metal.

He held his wrist to the headlamp. 'Lord, I must fly. I'm booked to appear at this smoker and it starts at 9.'

Dr Parry, who boasted a well-trained baritone, was in great demand at all local functions.

'All my young men,' said Penelope, with a toss of her pretty head, 'seem to prefer the smoking concert to me this evening.' Then, afraid she might have said too much, she asked quickly: 'Have you any new songs?'

'You know I haven't,' was his reproachful reply. 'You never seem to find time to try any over with me any more.' Rather viciously he kicked the bike into action. 'And you wouldn't let me stay here with you this evening, even if Aunt Emma would, and I hadn't a concert to go to. Good night, lovely Penny!'

'Good night, David!'

He went roaring into the mist.

II

After the chilly dampness outside, it was warm and snug in Mrs Farland's big bedroom above the porch on the first floor. In a pink silk negligée the invalid sat propped up among her cushions and knitted. Beside the bed Millie Pink was reading aloud from the evening paper, floundering and fumbling badly: at its foot Li Ho, the Peke, a black and brown ball in his basket, slumbered amid gentle, asthmatic snores.

'Who was that at the front just now?' Mrs Farland demanded brusquely as Penelope entered.

Millie Pink tittered. 'We're not used to gentlemen callers in the evening *here*, are we, dear Aunt Emma?'

'It was only Dr Parry,' Penelope replied,

ignoring this sally and addressing the woman in the bed. 'He brought a new bottle of cachets Father left for you.'

'Don't leave the bottle there, child!' snapped Mrs Farland, as Penelope placed the bottle on the bedside table. 'Millie, put it where it belongs—in the medicine cupboard in the dressing-room!'

This apartment, the exclusive domain for twenty years of married life of the late Mr Farland, opened off the bedroom. Millie picked up the bottle and disappeared.

'You're looking ever so much better, Mrs Farland,' said Penelope, sitting down in Millie's chair and taking the invalid's hand.

Emma Farland sniffed. 'I've my ups and downs. If I knew what was at the back of these pains I get—or who—I'd do better.' She spoke fretfully and glared in answer to the girl's frank and friendly gaze. 'You're not very pretty tonight, Penelope. Where's John?'

Penelope bore it with a smile. Feminine intuition had long since informed her of Mrs Farland's jealousy of pretty women.

'At the Works' smoker. He'll be in later to fetch me.'

Mrs Farland nodded and picked up her knitting again. 'Well, read to me. It's the interview with the luggage porter—Tadman, or whatever the stupid fellow's name is—about Nurse Ponting's arrival at Creepe station ...'

She raised her voice sharply. 'Millie, what are you doing in there all this time? You know I don't allow anyone to meddle with my medicines.'

Millie emerged hastily from the dressing-room. 'I thought I'd just tidy the cupboard a little.'

'That's the maid's duty, not yours. Go to bed. Penelope will read to me. At least she can enunciate her words clearly.'

Millie had a look of Christian forbearance which she reserved for Mrs Farland's more trying moments. It involved looking down her nose and pinching her lips together. She assumed it now, at the same time gently pressing the invalid's arm.

'Good night, Aunt Emma,' she murmured in honeyed tones and adding to Penelope, 'don't forget her Benger's at ten!' tiptoed out.

The travelling clock beside the bed marked the hour at ten minutes past nine. Penelope resumed her reading. The Haynes *Evening Chronicle*, a chastely pink sheet, had fairly let itself go about what it called 'The Junction Mystery'. A reporter had even travelled out to Whitestones and there were interviews, not only with Mrs Farland, but somewhat to the invalid's chagrin, with Millie Pink as well. Millie had already read these out to her aunt, but Penelope had to read them out again.

Presently, however, Mrs Farland's interest

77

waned, and her head drooped. Penelope put the paper aside. It was pleasant just to sit there and listen to the little night sounds of the country.

She must have dozed a little. A faint noise in the adjacent dressing-room aroused her—it sounded like the chink of bottles being moved. On its far side the dressing-room had a door which led to a landing where the bathroom was situated with a back staircase leading down. She thought it might be a maid; but the door communicating with the bedroom was ajar and the dressing-room was dark.

'Is that you, Agnes?' she called, softly so as not to awaken the woman in the bed.

When there was no reply she got up and moved towards the dressing-room. As she did so her ear caught another sound, faint but unmistakable—it was the sound of the other door, the door leading to the landing, being gently closed.

The light switch was just inside the dressing-room. She switched on the light. The room was empty. Everything was in order, the mahogany chest of drawers, the heavy mahogany clothes press, the white medicine cupboard above the fitted wash-basin. She hurried to the other door and, as she plucked it open, heard a step creak faintly on the descending flight.

For a moment she paused, frightened, impressed by the eeriness of that cautious and

78

sinister footfall in the darkness. She wanted to call out and ask who was there, but some instinct told her not to. Gathering her courage at last, she crept down the stairs.

The hall was empty when she reached it. The light was dim, and the shadows seemed somehow threatening. Then suddenly she heard the footfalls again, and her heart began pounding. They were outside the house now—footsteps creeping over the gravel.

Going into the unlighted dining-room, she stared through the window, putting her face close to the glass and cupping her hands.

She almost cried out, and she felt a strange cold thrill going through her.

There was a man outside the window, creeping away from the house, and though it was dark and she could see him only as a black silhouette, he was a man she knew so well that she recognised him immediately.

She watched until the darkness concealed him, then turned away and went upstairs again. She went up breathlessly, shaken by a horrible doubt, a ghastly suspicion, so terrible that she dared not admit it even to herself.

III

When she entered the bedroom again Mrs Farland was awake.

'I must have dropped off,' she remarked. 'Is it time for my Benger's, child?'

Penelope glanced at the clock. It was ten minutes to ten. 'I'll warm it up,' she said and, going to the fireplace, put a match to the gas-ring that stood there. Then she crossed to the dressing-room and opened the medicine cupboard. The bottle of Sleepine stood there on the shelf. She took the top cachet into her hand and returned to the bedside.

The saucepan bubbled gently on the hearth. The invalid fastened sharply suspicious eyes on Penelope as the girl, slim and graceful, shook up the pillows and smoothed out the eiderdown. 'Can you remember to remind Walton that I'm expecting him tomorrow?' she demanded suddenly.

'He hasn't forgotten, Mrs Farland. He's coming out to you after lunch.'

'He tells you all his secrets, I suppose?' Her tone was full of malice.

Penelope laughed. 'I'm very sure he doesn't, Mrs Farland.'

'Did he tell you I'd put Millie back in my will?'

The girl coloured. 'You know perfectly well that Mr Walton wouldn't dream of revealing a thing like that to anyone, even his private secretary.'

Mrs Farland sniffed. 'I had my doubts about Millie and cut her out. Then I put her back

80

again for nearly everything. But now—what do you suppose,' she exploded angrily, 'she wanted at my medicine cupboard tonight?'

'She was only tidying it, Mrs Farland.'

The invalid sniffed again. 'I wonder.' She paused. 'These mysterious pains of mine, this continual sickness, there must be some reason.' Gazing intently at the girl, she added: 'Don't you think it odd that it was Millie who discovered Nurse Ponting yesterday?'

'No. She just happened to be at the station, that's all.'

'You know of the part Nurse Ponting played in the Heaviside case?'

'Of course. It's in the paper.'

'I know—I know. But are you aware that Millie comes from Carlisle?'

'From Carlisle?'

'Where the Heavisides lived. Her father's a chemist there—or was, before he went bankrupt. He married my sister Ethel—she's in her grave these many years.'

The girl took the invalid's thin hand, fondled it. 'And you think that poor Millie—really, Mrs Farland, it's downright wrong to have such dreadful thoughts about anyone. You know,' she added mischievously, 'at one time I believe you suspected John.'

'It was his own fault. He cares nothing for me, only for the money he'll come into at my death.'

Mrs Farland's eyes were glaring at her.

'It's not true,' Penelope broke in hotly. 'If you think that, you don't know my John.' She plucked her hand away.

'There, there, child' the invalid said grudgingly. 'I'll admit he's been more attentive since he became engaged to you. Though what difference a girl like you could make to a young man as sure of himself as John is...'

'Your Benger's is boiling over,' said Penelope shortly and went to the fireplace.

She brought the cup to the bedside and held out the cachet. Obediently, the invalid gulped it down, then lay back relaxed on her pillows. Sipping the hot drink she remarked presently: 'When I do die, there'll be surprises—pleasant surprises for some people, unpleasant for others. But I'm not going to die yet. Go on with your reading.'

Once or thrice, in the ensuing half-hour, Penelope glanced over the top of the newspaper to see whether the patient was still awake. But always the sharp eyes were open and it was not until nearly eleven o'clock that Mrs Farland stopped her and said: 'I think I'll settle down for the night now. Put the bell-push by me so that I can ring for Millie if I want her. Good night, child!'

The windows were already open at the top. The girl switched off the bedside lamp and moved noiselessly to the door. As she opened it she came face to face with Millie who was rapidly backing away—Millie in a pink flannel dressing-gown and her hair twisted into a lot of little pig-tails.

'I was just coming to see that everything was all right,' Millie murmured and added, 'John hasn't arrived yet. Come and sit in my room while you're waiting.'

She led Penelope down the stairs to her bare and draughty bedroom beside the conservatory. The gas fire was lit and the two sat down before it.

'What was she saying about me a while back?' Millie asked rather tensely.

Penelope lifted an indifferent shoulder. 'Isn't there a proverb about listeners?'

Millie crimsoned. 'I wasn't listening. I just happened to be passing on my way back from the bath and heard her mention my name.' She broke off and said anxiously: 'Does she mean to take me out of her will again?'

'I'm afraid I don't know anything about it,' was the rather cold reply.

The other nodded darkly, warming her hands at the fire. 'You mean, you're not interested. After all, why should you be? When she dies John comes into his money and you'll marry him.' She stopped and raised her head. 'That's John now!'

The sound of wheels was audible on the gravel outside. They heard John's cheerful:

'Thanks for the lift, Harry!' and another voice reply: 'Good night, old man!'

Penelope ran downstairs. John was just letting himself in with his key. He swung the girl off her feet and held her close to him, then kissed her, long and tenderly, on the mouth.

'You're early, aren't you?' she said.

'Harry Keats from Yowle gave me a lift. How's Aunt Emma tonight?'

'Ever so much better and asleep.'

'Good. Then let's go into the dining-room and see if Agnes left me a sandwich. I could do with a drink, too—I'm frozen.'

There were sandwiches under a napkin on the sideboard. Penelope refused whisky but let him give her a glass of ginger ale. He mixed himself a whisky-and-soda and bore it to where she had seated herself on the padded rail surrounding the dying fire. Putting his drink untasted on the mantelshelf, he opened wide his arms.

Sweetly she surrendered to his embrace. Almost reverently he kissed his way from the back of her hand, the length of her arm, to the little golden tendrils that curled from the nape of her full, white neck.

'Darling,' he murmured, 'I seem to die when I'm away from you. Sweetness, tell me you feel the same about me.'

'You know I do,' she told him gravely, lying back in his arms, her face raised to his. She liked everything about this man, she told herself, as tenderly he drew her to him, the crispness of his dark hair, the whiteness of his teeth when he smiled, the fine air of fitness and virility he seemed to radiate, the caressing timbre of his voice when, like this, they were alone together. With eagerness she gave him back his kiss.

'Like me a little?' he murmured as, with a contented sigh, she pillowed her golden head on his chest.

'A whole lot.'

'Still want to marry me?'

'I'm counting the days.'

His nod was rather sombre. 'I feel that way about it, too. Poor Aunt Emma, I think she realizes it. That's why she's so certain I'm trying to do away with her.'

Penelope sighed. 'Isn't it awful to think that we must wait for her to die before we can be truly happy! ... Hark—there's her bell.'

From the upper regions an electric bell had suddenly shattered the stillness about them.

'Let Millie answer it!' he said. 'I haven't seen you for almost a week—why do you want to rush away now?' He shot her a frowning glance. 'Your friend, Dr Parry, was out here tonight, wasn't he?'

'He brought Mrs Farland her cachets.'

He nodded sombrely. 'He told me at the concert he'd seen you. Did the fellow try and

85

make love to you again?'

'He knows that that's all over and done with. It's idiotic of you to be jealous of David, John.'

His shrug was sulky. 'I'm not jealous—I object to the fellow, that's all. And he hates me. He's hated me ever since we blackballed him at the Conservative Club as an out-and-out Bolshie.'

She sighed. 'David's all right and the panel patients worship him. He talks nonsense sometimes, that's all.' To change the subject she said: 'Mrs Farland was going on about Millie again tonight. She's more than ever convinced that Millie's trying to poison her, simply because it was Millie who found Nurse Ponting yesterday.'

He wagged his head shrewdly. 'It certainly looks a bit odd. If there's anything in this idea of Aunt Emma's, nobody could polish her off more conveniently than Millie. After all, she's in continual attendance on Aunt Emma, gives her her medicine and so on. If Millie has really been up to anything, she can't have much liked the idea of a trained nurse, like this Nurse Ponting, and a poison expert at that, butting in. And, you know, Pen, Millie hates Aunt Emma with a deadly hate. It's not surprising, the way my Aunt treats her, always monkeying about with that will of hers. I wonder what Millie would say if she knew that Walton's coming here tomorrow to cut her out of the will again.'

86

The girl looked rather scared. 'For mercy's sake, John, don't let on to Mrs Farland that I told you. If Mr Walton knew that I'd been gossiping outside the office, he'd fire me on the spot.'

'All right. I won't give you away,' John said.

Penelope smiled at him in a strange way.

'You talk about the hatred between Millie and Aunt Emma, but do you never realize that Aunt Emma hasn't much use for me either.'

'That's just her way,' John answered uneasily. 'I'm sure she doesn't hate you. Who could?'

'I'm not so sure of it, John. You see...'

The words died on her lips as the door was violently flung open. Millie was there in her pink wrapper, breathless, almost hysterical.

'Aunt Emma,' she panted, 'she's got another of her attacks, the worst she's had yet. She's been most dreadfully sick. We'd better get your father to her, Penelope.'

A long, wailing scream welled into the hush of the dining-room.

'Oh, my God!' cried Millie.

Without speaking John Farland sprang up and hurried out, the two women following. The invalid was tossing in her bed, her hands clasped to her stomach, groaning piteously. From time to time with horrible effect, her groans rose shrilly to a shriek. Her face, glistening with perspiration, was the colour of clay, her eyes were closed, her mouth twitched. She was barely conscious, and when Farland spoke to her, paid no heed but continued to moan and rock herself about in the bed.

'I gave her the rest of the Benger's and another cachet,' Millie declared, 'but, oh, dear, the poor thing doesn't seem able to keep anything down. Her cachets have usually helped her before. She's allowed up to three—maybe, we'd best give her a third. We could break it up in a spoonful of brandy.'

The new bottle of Sleepine, freshly opened, was on the bedside table. Penelope shook out a cachet while Millie ran to the dressing-room for the brandy. 'I'll go and ring your father,' John told Penelope.

'Unless he's back from Cobling, you won't get him,' the girl replied. 'The Morrisons, where he's gone, aren't on the telephone. If Daddy isn't home, you'd better call Dr Parry. He has the 'phone at his rooms—Creepe 117.'

The young man nodded and hurried out. Penelope ran out after him to the top of the stairs. 'When you've done telephoning, take the car and fetch Nurse Cran,' she yelled. 'You know where she lives in the village!'

'All right!' He waved his hand and disappeared under the stairs where the telephone stood.

The patient's screams had aroused the house. Agnes appeared, wearing a raincoat over her nightdress, and Mrs Burch, the cook, in a shawl with her hair in papers. Another violent attack of nausea was shaking the invalid when Penelope returned to the bedroom. Presently, as the invalid lay back exhausted among her pillows, she raised terrified eyes to Penelope who bent over her.

'I feel as if I were on fire,' she groaned feebly. 'All my inside's burning.' She began to scream again.

Finding that the patient's feet were 'stone cold,' as she put it, Millie despatched Agnes to fill the hot water bottle afresh. Mrs Farland's face was assuming a pinched look and the shrewd, sharp eyes, when after a little she opened them on Penelope, were dull and lifeless.

'This weakness,' she gasped, 'I think—I'm going—to die!' Her head dropped forward on her chest.

So Nurse Cran, summarily attired in gum boots and a shabby ulster, found her when, in about twenty minutes' time, she bustled into the room. Dr Cheedle was still out, Farland, who appeared with the nurse, whispered to Penelope, but Dr Parry was on his way. At the sight of the patient Nurse Cran's face changed. She felt the pulse and bade Millie brusquely to procure some hot coffee.

The coffee had not appeared and the invalid, sunk in a stertorous coma, had ceased to groan or toss, when the clatter of a motor-cycle was audible outside. It was David Parry, his rubber overalls bespattered with mud. 'Sorry I was so long,' he said, 'but I ran out of petrol.' For a moment he stooped over the bed, then turned back to the chair where he had placed his bag, found a hypodermic needle and proceeded to fill it. During this operation, 'She's very low,' he said in an undertone to Farland, who stood at his side. He advanced to the bed and made the injection, then, drawing up a chair, sat down to watch.

Out of the silence of the countryside a bell tolled faintly twelve times. It was midnight sounding from Yowle Church. John Farland and Penelope with linked hands stood at the foot of the bed, Millie Pink at their side, beyond her Nurse Cran.

'How did this attack start?' Dr Parry demanded. He addressed no one in particular, speaking over his shoulder.

Millie replied, telling how, answering Mrs Farland's bell, soon after eleven o'clock, she had found the patient restless and agitated and complaining of thirst and burning pains and extreme nausea. She described how she had administered a second cachet of Sleepine.

Dr Parry picked up the Sleepine bottle from the table at his side. 'This is the new bottle, eh? The one I brought tonight.'

'Yes, Doctor,' said Millie.

'I gave her a cachet with her Benger's at ten,' Penelope explained.

'Dr Cheedle said she might have up to three cachets if she was restless and in pain at any time,' Millie put in. 'Penelope and I broke up the third in a spoonful of brandy for her before Nurse Cran arrived. But it only seemed to make her worse.'

The doctor frowned and, leaning forward, lifted the patient's eyelid. 'It's as I feared, she's collapsed,' he said with a shake of the head. 'She doesn't react to any stimulus.'

The brakes of a car screamed, tyres churned the gravel, beneath the window. The front door bell shrilled. A moment later Agnes ushered in Dr Cheedle. He looked utterly exhausted. 'Ah, John,' he said wearily, 'I found your message when I got in.'

Dr Parry was stooping over the bed. He straightened up and met his partner face to face as Dr Cheedle approached the bed.

'I'm sorry,' he said with a shrug, and stepped aside. 'She died just as you arrived.'

With an exclamation the older man pushed past him and in a deathly silence made a rapid examination.

Dr Parry was staring at the Sleepine bottle which he held in his hands.

'This isn't the bottle I brought out here tonight!' he exclaimed.

Dr Cheedle took the bottle from him. 'My dear fellow, you don't know what you're talking about. This is the bottle I left out for you and there's the maker's name on it.'

The other shook his head obstinately. 'The bottle I brought had a little nick on the inside of the neck. I remember noticing it and wondering whether I should change it, lest any broken glass had got mixed up with the capsules.' He thrust out his jaw. 'This is not the bottle I handed to Penelope, Cheedle, and that's final!'

NOTES

1. I am filled with admiration at the skill with which Miss Dorothy Sayers has laid the foundation of the story and the ingenuity with which Mr Freeman Wills Crofts has picked up the threads.

2. I like the idea of John Farland, as a false hero, being the real murderer and have adopted in toto F.W.C.'s scheme by which Farland contrived to do away with Nurse Ponting.

3. The fact remains, however, that, at a comparatively early stage in the story, D.S. and F.W.C. have landed me, as furnisher of Part III, with two murders on my hands—my reading of the two instalments before mine being that (*a*) Mrs Farland is being poisoned by arsenic and (*b*) that the poisoner is also the murderer of Nurse Ponting.

4. As the story sets out with the strong indication that Mrs Farland is being poisoned, it seems to me that her murder is the main crime and the murder of Nurse Ponting secondary.

5. I see John Farland's modus operandi (in the matter of poisoning Aunt Emma) as follows. If he left his bottle of Sleepine pills treated with arsenic *permanently* in the medicine cupboard (F.W.C.'s Notes—John Farland), it would mean that *every time* Aunt Emma took a cachet, she would have a seizure of varying violence. My idea is that from time to time on his visits to Whitestones, he substitutes his bottle of poison cachets for the real one and, when the patient has had her Benger's, replaces the poison bottle by the genuine one, to guard against the possibility of the contents of the bottle being analysed.

6. However, during the week preceding Mrs Farland's death (the first week of January—see Sayers, page 10), he was anxious to finish the old lady off and left the bottle of arsenic pills, prepared, as F.W.C. indicates, with the heaviest doses at the bottom, in the medicine cupboard. Intentionally he remains away from Whitestones and so is unaware of the fact that Mrs Farland has been taking two and even three cachets daily instead of her

93

customary one and that his poison bottle is down to the last cachet. It might be explained that, for a day or two before the fatal Monday night, Mrs Farland had taken it into her head to refuse to take her Sleepine which would account for the improvement in her condition on the day of her death.

7. It is only at the smoking concert on the Monday night that Farland discovers from Dr Parry that (*a*) there is only one cachet left in the poison bottle, and (*b*) that Parry has just taken out a new genuine bottle to Whitestones. Farland had anticipated that the poison capsules he had left would have sufficed to do the trick, and had contemplated incriminating Millie Pink as he knew from Penelope that Mrs F. was about to cut Millie out of her will again. Penelope denied to Mrs Farland knowing anything of Walton's affairs. But she was his secretary and she was aware of his appointment with Mrs Farland on the following day and its purpose. She told John about it when they met for a few minutes on the Monday evening when he agreed to lend her his Austin for her trip out to Whitestones.

8. At the smoker Farland realises that his plot is in jeopardy—the sooner he can finish off Mrs Farland, the more surely will Millie be

suspected. He has no car and Whitestones is 10 miles away. Therefore, while Parry is waiting his turn to appear at the concert, John clandestinely borrows the latter's motor-bike which has been left outside the hall and speeds out to Whitestones and changes the full bottle which Parry has left for a new one, afterwards returning to the concert.

Time-table

Parry leaves Whitestones after delivering Sleepine	9.00 p.m.
Arrives concert (Creepe)	9.25 p.m.
John on Parry's bike leaves concert	9.30 p.m.
Arrives Whitestones	9.45 p.m.
Leaves Whitestones	9.50 p.m.
Arrives back at concert	10.05 p.m.
Leaves concert with Harry Keats who gives him a lift to Whitestones	10.50 p.m.
Arrives Whitestones	11.15 p.m.

9. It was Farland whom Penelope heard chinking bottles about in the dressing-room at about 9.45 p.m.

10. It had been John's intention, once the poisoned cachets had been administered, to replace the poison bottle by the genuine one which he had kept in his pocket. But at the last moment he wavered, perceived what a perfect opportunity for in-

95

criminating Millie Pink the poison bottle afforded and before he could decide what to do Dr Parry had arrived and impounded the poison bottle.

11. I have the impression that Inspector Billingham will soon arrive at the conclusion, while pursuing his investigations into the murder of Nurse Ponting, that the murderer of Nurse Ponting and Mrs Farland is one and the same person and that, once he can get a reasonable line as to the identity of Mrs Farland's murderer, all the component parts of his investigation into the Ponting case will slip smoothly into place.

General Observations

A. Having plumped for F.W.C.'s choice of Farland as the murderer of both Nurse Ponting and Aunt Emma, I do not feel that Farland can provide the suitable love interest, nor am I much excited by the possibilities of P.C. Bratton (see Miss Sayers' Notes VII).

I have therefore ventured to build up Dr Cheedle's partner, Dr (David) Parry, as Penelope's ultimate love interest, a struggling young doctor from some cheap provincial University, honest-minded, infused with a furious indignation over the plight of the poor, and desperately in love with Penelope. I see him, after a period of being suspected by Inspector Billingham, placing his common sense and scientific knowledge at the Inspector's disposal for the unmasking of the real murderer.

B. To link Penelope up more closely with the plot, I have made her private secretary to Walton the solicitor. To my mind this had certain advantages, to wit (*a*) She is a direct pipe-line for John into the Walton office and so into Aunt Emma's intentions regarding her will. It is also from her that John hears of Walton's proposal to engage Nurse Ponting and of the nurse's connection with the Heavisides case: she writes him every day and conveys this information in a note she sends round by the surgery boy on Saturday afternoon; (*b*) It suggests that Dr Cheedle is not particularly well-off and that Penelope's marriage to John and Aunt Emma's death might relieve him from some considerable money difficulties (money-lenders?).

My instalment concludes with the death of Mrs Farland and Dr Parry's blunt announcement that the Sleepine bottle has been changed. What directed Parry's attention to the bottle were the obvious symptoms of arsenic poisoning. Who switched the bottle?

The Suspects

Millie Pink

(*a*) She hates Mrs Farland; (*b*) She fears she is to be cut out of the will again; (*c*) Penelope heard someone at the medicine cupboard in the dressing-room soon after Millie had been sent to bed; (*d*) Penelope found Millie listening at the door; (*e*) Millie comes from Carlisle, the scene of the Heavisides trial (Nurse Ponting); (*f*) Millie's father is a chemist suggesting (1) that he might have been concerned in the Heavisides case and (2) that Millie had some secret access to poison drugs; (*g*) Millie discovered Nurse Ponting dying at Creepe Station.

Dr Parry

He is alleged to hate Farland who had him black-balled, and Farland is known to be the most important beneficiary under Mrs Farland's will. Did Parry leave the poison bottle when he came at 9 p.m. and then, to avert suspicion from himself, publicly announce that the bottle has been changed? Was it Parry Penelope saw creeping away from the house after she had caught the sound of someone moving about in the dressing-room?

Penelope

Is she John Farland's accomplice or her father's? It was she who administered the cachet that brought on Mrs Farland's first attack. She knew Nurse Ponting's history. Was she really out on the Sunday afternoon?

I have not had the space to develop Miss Sayers' vague suspicions against Dr Cheedle; but if he is shown to be in money difficulties, his daughter might be suspected of having, on his orders, brought with her to Whitestones the poison bottle to substitute for the one that Parry left.

John Farland
He had the run of the house, also a latch-key. Was his presence at the smoker missed between the hours of 9.30 p.m. and 10.05 p.m.? Does the heavy clay on the tyres of his Austin correspond to the mud of the 'deserted wood'? (see F.W.C.'s Notes, under 'John Farland.') Why did Dr Parry run out of petrol on his second trip to Whitestones by motor bike? The answer is that he had not allowed for the supplementary 20 miles that Farland had covered on the borrowed bike—the point might have importance in ultimately bringing the murder home to Farland.

PART FOUR

by F. Tennyson Jesse

The white dawn brought no cheer to Whitestones. The laurels, depressing enough bushes at the best of times, and the sweep of gravel drive, were dark with damp. The old-fashioned striped red-and-white blinds pulled down over every window gave the square, solid, Victorian house an incongruous air of being decked with gigantic sugar-sticks. The only sign of life from without was the smoke crawling languidly up from the kitchen chimney, for the living have to eat no matter who lies dead.

Penelope had not gone home. The servants were pleasurably agitated in the kitchen—a death in the house is always exciting, and when that death may be murder ... Murder. The very word had a ring of not altogether repulsive horror.

'It may be our turn next,' said old Agnes darkly, as she waited while Cook made the early morning tea: 'Such goings on!'

'Well, I've always and ever said doctors was too free with all their nasty drugs,' said Cook. 'Stands to reason accidents is bound to happen sometimes. And that is what you will find it was, Agnes. Just an accident. Who'd have wanted to do her in?'

'I've always been with real gentry. I'm not used to having this sort of thing in the house. My Mum'll be ever so upset when she knows,' said Florence.

'There's others will be worse upset yet,' prophesied Agnes, still in her sibylline mood. 'After all, when a death's not natural—and this wasn't natural, Cook, say what you will—*someone* has had a hand in it.'

'Well, I'm sure it couldn't have been Mr John,' cried Florence, on whom that young man's pleasant manners and good looks had made an impression.

'Nor Miss Millie. She wouldn't have the guts,' said Cook tersely.

'Perhaps she went and took it herself, just to make a fuss, like,' said young Edie, the kitchen-maid.

'Now, Edie,' said Cook sharply, annoyed at this expression of opinion from a social inferior. 'Have you got nothing to do but sit there? Take Mr John's tray up.'

'I'll take it,' said Florence. 'She can take Miss Millie's. Oh, I wonder where Miss Penelope is. She didn't go home, did she?'

'She's in the dining-room and ready for her breakfast,' said Cook, in the pleasant position of being the one who knew most in her own kitchen. 'She's got a healthy appetite, bless her.

101

She's looking fresh as a daisy. I'm going to fry her some bacon and eggs.'

And that most pleasant of domestic incense, the smell of bacon frying, duly went up into the air.

Penelope was, indeed, hungry for her breakfast. It had been a trying night. Her father and Dr Parry had locked the room where Mrs Farland lay dead and taken the key with them. At any moment Inspector Billingham, who had begun a preliminary investigation on the previous night, was expected to return and take statements from her, from Millie, from John, the two doctors, even from the servants. Already, although no suspicions had been fixed, there was, as it were, floating in the air, she felt, a suspicion that John Farland or Millie must have had something to do with the death of their extremely tiresome aunt. It was common knowledge that John was the heir and common gossip that she had intended to change her will.

Cook, who with her own hands bore in the eggs and bacon, thought Mr John a very lucky man, even if one of them doctors (and one of them the girl's own father!) had made up a prescription wrongly. Yes, there was a girl for you! Penelope looked up and smiled as the old woman poured out her coffee for her and set the eggs and bacon in front of her.

'Oh, Cook, you're an angel,' said Penelope. 'I'm so hungry. Yes, I'm as hungry as I am at a funeral, when for some extraordinary reason one never can stop eating.'

'I had a sister who was like that. But she was funny that way. Give her a funeral for eating at before a wedding any day, she always said.'

'It's nerves, I suppose,' said Penelope. 'But it makes one feel frightfully indecent somehow. I shouldn't be eating this.'

'You eat it, dearie,' said Cook. 'Somebody has to keep their strength up. Miss Millie won't be much good.'

'No. Poor Millie,' said Penelope thoughtfully. 'Well, thanks very much, Cook. I'll eat this as quickly as I can. I expect we'll have a lot of questions asked of us.'

Cook took the hint and went back into the kitchen. As Penelope was finishing her breakfast John came into the room. He was looking a little better than he had the night before, for he had bathed and shaved, but he was still very haggard. Penelope looked up at him and laughed, her beautiful frank laugh that never failed to stir him.

'Darling, I know what you are thinking,' she said. 'That it's positively indecent of me to be eating, but I was *so* hungry! Have you had anything?'

'I've had some tea. I can't eat,' said John. 'Oh, Penelope, thank Heaven for people like you. There's nobody like you in the whole world. Millie's just a sobbled mess by now, and my head's in such a muddle I can't even sort things out myself. I feel as though I were in the middle of a frightful nightmare and would wake up and find it's none of it true. Damn it all, it's not the sort of thing that happens—not to people like us, anyway.'

Penelope had been busy filling her cup with good strong coffee again, and now she brought it over to John.

'Drink this, darling. It'll do more good than eating, if you don't mind sharing my cup.'

John's face broke into his first smile since the trouble had come upon them the previous evening.

'Share your cup, Penelope! It sounds like a dream of bliss. All I want to do is to share everything with you. You know that.'

'Yes, darling, of course I do. But I am rather glad Inspector Billingham can't hear you say it.'

John drank the coffee and lit a cigarette and felt a little better. He drew up his chair to the table and sat facing Penelope, his chin on his hands.

'I'm not going to sit beside you, for I should hold your hand, or kiss you, and then I shouldn't be able to think. Now, let's try and straighten out this nightmare.'

'I don't know that we can yet,' said Penelope. 'That's the trouble of it. Anyway, we don't know for certain how your aunt died. There's been no post-mortem yet. But suppose, John, just suppose ... we find she's been ...' she hesitated for a moment and then brought the word out bravely ... 'murdered. Well—then?'

'Yes,' said John, 'well then ... everyone will look at me and Millie, I suppose.'

Penelope was playing with her coffee-spoon, and she remained silent for a moment, then raised her eyes to him—deep clear blue eyes that looked very straightly at him.

'John,' she said, 'don't be shocked, but are you ... are you absolutely sure of Millie?'

'Sure of Millie? What do you mean?'

'Sure that she didn't ... sure that she wouldn't have ... Your aunt gave her a frightful life of it, you know.'

'Good God!' said John violently. 'I'm as sure of Millie as I am of myself.'

'Not for the same reasons, though,' pointed out Penelope. 'You are sure of yourself, A: because you know you didn't do it, B: because you know you couldn't do it. But you're only sure of Millie because you think she couldn't have.'

'She hasn't the guts,' said John, repeating, had he known it, what Cook had said in the kitchen.

'A rat, or for the matter of that, even a mouse, driven into a corner, has an amazing amount of guts,' said Penelope. She got up and went round the table, and standing behind him laid her hands on his shoulders.

'John,' she said, 'don't you know that whatever happens you must be kept clear of this? Injustices *do* happen in the world—frightful injustices, and it's true you may be suspected. Well, I'd throw Millie and anybody else in the world down the drain for you, and you know it.'

'Not if they were innocent,' said John quietly.

'But someone must be guilty,' pointed out Penelope.

'You don't ask me whether I am or not,' said John.

'No,' said Penelope pressing his head against her and beginning to smooth his hair back from his forehead. 'I don't ask you, John. That would be silly and absurd.'

John caught her hand, putting it to his lips.

'There's Daddy coming,' said Penelope. 'Everything is going to begin all over again.'

John got to his feet and for a moment they clung together silently, and then Penelope went and opened the front door to her father before he could ring the bell. The old man stumped wearily into the dining-room, threw his hat on the table and sank down into an arm-chair.

'Penelope,' he said, 'you had better get home, my dear; all sorts of unpleasant things have got to happen. We have got to get Mrs Farland out of the house to the mortuary; there's an inquest to be fixed; Billingham will be here any moment, and there's going to be a devil of a tamasha.'

Dr Cheedle, during the War, had served in India and some of the phrases of the life of the pukka sahib still clung to him. They were, so to speak, his invisible war medals.

'I won't go home,' said Penelope, 'except for a bath and change. You forget I'm a working girl. I'm going along to Mr Walton as usual. I expect there will be a lot of work to be done. Besides, the Inspector'll want to see me.'

The eyes of the old man were lit with a tender pride and affection as he looked at the girl.

'Yes, he will,' he replied. 'And you'll do whatever you think best, I don't doubt. Hullo! Who is that coming up in a taxi?'

'It's the station taxi,' said Penelope, 'And it's got luggage on it. Why, there's a girl getting out.'

They all three stood, hidden themselves, looking out from behind the shelter of the white lace curtains.

'She's keeping the taxi, whoever she is,' observed John. The door bell rang and John made a movement as though to answer it and then stopped.

'Better let Florence go,' observed Penelope, who had detained him by the lightest touch on his arm. 'We have got to behave in as ordinary a way as possible for today and probably for many days. You mustn't answer doors, John.'

107

'Oh, God,' grunted John. 'What a life!'

They heard Florence's quick step across the hall, the opening of the front door and a murmur of voices. Then Florence came into the room.

'It's a young lady. She asked for Mrs Farland. I told her she couldn't see her.'

'Did you say she was dead?' said John.

'I said she had passed away,' replied Florence reprovingly. 'So she asked if she could see anyone else of the family. I think she wants to see you, Mr John.'

'All right,' said John. 'Show her in here. What's her name, by the way?'

'Miss Joan Cliff, she said her name was.'

The three in the dining-room looked blankly at each other. The name said nothing to any of them.

'Show her in,' repeated John impatiently.

'Miss Cliff,' announced Florence, and withdrew very reluctantly, shutting the door after her.

The girl who entered was not very noticeable except to the discriminating eye. She was small and slight. The soft waves of her brown hair blended with the brown of the little hat, which, like all self-respecting girls of the moment, she wore adhering to her right ear. Her eyes, big, dark, and long-lashed, were her most noticeable feature, and her bones were very small and fine, and she moved beautifully. But set against the

108

blazing beauty of Penelope she might have passed for a sparrow beside a bird of paradise. She stood hesitating for a moment and then advanced towards John.

'You, I think,' she said, 'must be Mr Farland. I am so sorry to bother you on an occasion like this, but I'd no idea your aunt had died till the maid told me.'

She had a soft voice, the sort that John had called to himself when he was a little boy a 'dark voice'.

'She died last night. We are all rather—upset,' said John. 'This is Dr Cheedle and Miss Penelope Cheedle. And you?'

'I'm Nurse Ponting's niece. Dr Walton telephoned me last night and I caught the earliest train there was this morning.'

'Have you had breakfast?' said Penelope quickly.

'No.'

'Well, you must have some fresh coffee and toast.' And she went quickly to the door and opened it, finding (as she expected) Florence standing on the other side.

'There's no need for you to be waiting about outside the door, Florence,' said Penelope dryly. 'Ask Cook to make some fresh toast and coffee and bring it in for Miss Cliff.'

'Yes, Miss,' said Florence with unwonted meekness, her face a fiery red.

Penelope went back into the dining-room and

shut the door.

'It must have been the most frightful shock to you,' she said. 'I'm so sorry.'

The girl gave her a quick grateful smile.

'Yes, it was a shock, though of course Aunt Hilda wasn't well when she left London. I didn't think she ought to come. She'd not been well for some time, but she simply couldn't afford not to take a job, and she's a splendid nurse ... she *was*, I mean.' And Joan Cliff's lower lip began to quiver a little.

'There, there,' said Dr Cheedle, vaguely, patting her on the back. 'You were very fond of your aunt, I suppose?'

'She did everything for me,' said the girl. 'She brought me up. Her sister married my father, who was a doctor. He and my mother died in the Spanish influenza after the War.'

Dr Cheedle tut-tutted sympathetically and Penelope poured out fresh coffee which had arrived, and said firmly:

'Now you really must drink this.'

'She was wonderful,' said the girl. 'She really was, and people were often beastly to her because of ...' She hesitated, and stopped.

'Yes, yes,' said Dr Cheedle. 'I know—that case she was mixed up in. She told me. She was only doing her duty as a good citizen.'

'Of course she was,' cried Joan gratefully. A tinge of colour came into her cheeks. 'That was what I always told her. Of course she had a very

110

hard time of it, and what she would have done without Dr Walton's kindness I don't know. Things only really began to be easier when I could start earning.'

'And what do you do?' asked Penelope, buttering some toast.

'I'm a dispenser. Dr Walton helped again there. It's a very good job.'

John, who had been walking rather uneasily back and forth, now said:

'There's the Inspector. You'll have to meet him, I'm afraid, Miss Cliff.'

'I feel much better now, thanks to your coffee,' said the girl, smiling gratefully at Penelope.

Inspector Billingham came in, was introduced to the newcomer, and shook hands all round. Joan liked him at once. There was no Sherlock Holmesy air about him, she decided. She liked his quiet grey eyes and his clean scrubbed look.

'Well, this is a bad business,' said the Inspector, refusing coffee, but lighting a cigarette. 'The doctors—correct me if I'm wrong—think it more than likely Mrs Farland didn't die a natural death.'

Joan Cliff glanced up. For a moment it seemed she was going to speak, then she checked herself.

'I know they do,' said John, 'but all that *must* be nonsense. Who on earth would have done such a thing?'

'John dear,' said Penelope, 'it's no use going on like that. You had much better just wait and answer the questions the Inspector will ask you. You *have* come to ask us all questions, haven't you, Inspector?'

Instinctively Penelope ranged herself by John's side, touching his hand with hers. She's a good plucky 'un, the Inspector thought, although he kept his face impassive.

'Yes. I would like to see you each alone,' he replied. 'Just a mere matter of routine, you know.'

'Perhaps you would like to go into the smoking-room and we will come to you there.'

'That's a good idea, Miss Cheedle. If you'll come along now, we'll get the unpleasant job done as quickly as possible. And then Dr Cheedle, perhaps you will follow. You are a busy man, I know.'

'Certainly,' said Dr Cheedle. 'I am at your disposal. Dr Parry is looking after my patients this morning. He's expecting me as soon as I can relieve him.'

John held the door open and Penelope, with a reassuring smile at him, crossed the hall into the smoking-room. The Inspector shut the door and pulled out one of the big leather arm-chairs for Penelope, who fell into it gratefully. She suddenly realised she was very tired.

'Miss Cheedle,' Billingham said without any

preliminary, 'where were you on Sunday afternoon?'

He was watching her intently, and though she gave no palpable sign of alarm, he had the impression that she sort of cringed within herself as he asked the question.

'I was just out,' she said. 'I went walking.'

'In the rain?'

She flashed her radiant smile at him.

'Modern young women aren't afraid of rain, Inspector. If I want to go for a walk, a little rain won't stop me.'

'What time did you get back to your father's house?'

'I forget now.'

'In time to see Nurse Ponting?'

He saw the smile fade slowly from her face. She lowered her golden head for a moment, sat frowning and biting her lip.

Then she said in a low, serious voice:

'It's silly to try to deceive you, Inspector. I'd better tell you the truth. I didn't go out on Sunday afternoon. I was at home all the time.'

He became conscious of his heart leaping.

'Why did you pretend that you were out, Miss Cheedle—not only to me, but to Mr Farland?'

Her blue eyes lifted to his face again.

'It was because of Mr Farland. It's so awful that I'm afraid to tell you in case you get the wrong impression.'

'You've got to tell me, Miss Cheedle.'

'I—I know. Well,' she said, suddenly raising her voice a little, in desperation, 'my father knew that John was coming to the house to take me for a run in the car, and he didn't want him to meet Nurse Ponting.'

'Why not?'

'Because,' Penelope said, with an unexpected sob, 'John was one of the suspects, wasn't he? John and Millie between them.'

The Inspector stared at her, his brain turning over a mass of possibilities and suspicions. That explanation sounded plausible. Was it true?

Suddenly he remembered something in Dr Cheedle's statement.

'So your father *was* expecting the nurse to call that afternoon?'

She nodded. 'Yes. That's why he wanted me there. She had come on a long journey, and it's always a little awkward for a man with a woman he doesn't know. She might have wanted to wash or anything. But she wasn't there long. She had tea and then went.'

'*You* had tea with her?'

'Yes.'

'Why didn't you want to tell me that you'd been in the house all the time?'

'Because I didn't want John to know that I'd lied to him, of course—or, rather, that I'd allowed Father to.' She leant towards him. 'Please don't tell John unless you've got to,' she appealed. 'You can imagine how frightful it would seem to him if he knew. It looks as if Father and I felt certain that he was killing his aunt, and were engaged in a conspiracy to trap him.'

'Yes, I see that,' Billingham answered quietly, and he forced himself to smile at her. 'Well, I'll keep your secret if I can. The fact that you were at the house doesn't seem to be of much importance, anyway. But now tell me—of course, I'm not asking you to incriminate Mr Farland or anybody else—but what do you think about the matter in general? I mean, have you noticed anything that seems puzzling to you?'

She seemed relieved by this turn in the conversation—as he had intended her to be.

'There's one thing,' she said earnestly. 'I do think that Dr Parry was entirely wrong in saying it wasn't the same Sleepine bottle. It looked exactly the same to me.'

'Of course, you know your father's Sleepine bottles well by sight?'

'Oh, they look like any other bottles. You know, my father gave me Sleepine myself when I had 'flu a little while ago and couldn't sleep. They say if you hear of a thing once you hear of it three times. There was poor Nurse Ponting who took it, and me, and Mrs Farland. I never want to hear of the wretched stuff again.'

'I can quite understand,' said the Inspector

sympathetically. 'By the way, Nurse Ponting didn't take any Sleepine while she was with you at your house?'

Penelope shook her golden head.

'Not that I know of. She took several cachets out of a box—the box the Sleepine cachet was found in, but she told me it was a cold cure, and naturally I never thought twice about it.'

'Of course not,' agreed the Inspector. 'And she seemed quite all right when she left you?'

'Well, she seemed as all right as when she came in. She didn't like Daddy's China tea, you know, and he said: "Penelope likes that black poison brew herself. She'll give you a cup if you go up to her room." I was very anxious to meet her, of course, because I knew what she had been sent here for, and I liked her at once. She struck me as being an awfully nice woman, and I made her the tea and we chatted for ten minutes, and I told her that Mr Farland was going to call at the station for her, and she said she must be getting back to fetch her suitcase and that the walk would do her good. Then, of course, came the awful news that she was dead, so I came along to see if I couldn't help by sitting up with Mrs Farland. Millie was about worn out, and really, Inspector, there is nothing I can tell you about Mrs Farland except that Nurse Cran left, and Millie and I dined together and then Millie went up to be with Mrs Farland. I waited downstairs, and Dr Parry arrived with the new bottle of Sleepine. He went away, and I took it upstairs to Mrs Farland.'

'What did you do then?' asked the Inspector.

'Millie went to have a bath, and I read to Mrs Farland. Then Millie came back and . . .'

'Never mind about Miss Pink. What did *you* do?'

'Oh, I said good night to Mrs Farland and left her. I passed Millie on my way down here, and I sat and waited for John, and he came back and . . .' She stopped.

'Well?'

'Well, we sat and talked for quite a long time. I'm afraid we don't get much time together, Inspector.'

The Inspector reflected that his sympathies were with John Farland if he wanted to keep this beautiful creature by his side for as long as possible.

'Where did you sit?' he asked.

'In the dining-room. There were sandwiches, and John had a drink, and then suddenly Millie ran down and said that Mrs Farland was terribly ill. After that, it all seems the most dreadful muddle to me. Nurse Cran came back, and Dr Parry and then Daddy, and everyone was rushing about, but nothing was any good and Mrs Farland died.'

'Then the only thing,' said the Inspector, 'of any interest that you have to tell me is that you think Dr Parry was mistaken in saying the bottle was changed?'

'I am sure he was,' said Penelope. 'Besides, how could Millie have changed it? Why should she?'

'Come, come,' said the Inspector briskly. 'Nobody has suggested that it was Miss Pink who changed the bottle—provided that anyone *did*. Well, thank you very much, Miss Cheedle.' He got up and opened the door. 'Perhaps you will ask your father to come in, and after that Mr Farland, and then Miss Pink. And, by the way, who is the new young lady?'

'She's Joan Cliff,' said Penelope. 'She's Nurse Ponting's niece—a dispenser.'

When Penelope had left, the Inspector went over to the window and stood staring out at the dripping laurel bushes. He felt nervous and dejected.

So Penelope had seen Nurse Ponting on Sunday afternoon! Worse, she and the nurse had taken tea together alone. And Penelope was in the running for Mrs Farland's fortune. And Penelope had done her best just now to make him believe that the murderess was Millie Pink...

The Inspector was human enough to be aware of a swift hope that such a beautiful girl would not have killed two elderly women ... After all, he told himself, there's a hell of a lot of people in this who had access to drugs. Even that silly Miss Pink was science mistress at a school, John Farland was a big noise at the Chemical Works ... then there were two doctors and Joan Cliff the dispenser ... The whole business was a blinking chemist's shop. Why, unlikely as it might seem, even Joan Cliff, harmless as she looked, might have wanted to put her aunt out of the way, and the two murders might be unconnected after all. For, as the Inspector's long experience had told him, you never knew anything about people till you knew the secrets of their home life. And quiet insignificant-looking people could have strange skeletons in their apparently commonplace cupboards.

NOTES

I have come to the conclusion that the only thing more difficult than being the writer of the last chapter in this book, is being the writer of the fourth chapter. Miss Sayers presents me (who has never been able to read an A.B.C. Time-table) with masses of complicated trains. However, I am much too much of a fan of Miss Sayers to complain. Mr Freeman Wills Crofts, one of whose most ardent fans I also am, presents me with one or two things I really cannot swallow, such as the fact that a nurse, who has already been mixed up in a murder case, would accept a nasty cold drink in a nasty cold wood from a total stranger. Mr Valentine Williams, whose fan I am both as a reader and a friend, agrees with Mr Freeman Wills Crofts that it is a good idea to make John Farland the false hero. No. Here, my dear Valentine, and here, my two other predecessors, is where I leave you all very violently.

There is only one possible criminal in this book, by which I mean, only one who will really surprise the reader, but who, so far, has been in a position to do all the dirty work. The ingenious red-herrings of porters and station-masters laid by Miss Sayers are, I am sure, for our confusion. Whatever happens, we mustn't call coincidence to our aid. But there is one person on whom suspicion doesn't fall, and must not, until the last chapter, one who is in a position to have seen the nurse, to have given her the poison, to have known who she was and why she was being sent, to whom it was of the utmost importance that the old lady should die so that John might come into his inheritance, and that one person is—Penelope.

Let us remember that the old lady is poisoned by arsenic. No doctor poisons by arsenic—the 'Fool's Poison'—which clears Dr Cheedle and Dr Parry. It also clears John Farland who works at a chemical works. Arsenic is used because it is the only thing that the poor wretched lay-man, such as ourselves, can get hold of—just as nurses drink tea, poor wretches, because it is the only intoxicant they are allowed. It is most important, to my mind, not to violate human nature in a detective story.

Now there are very few thrills left in a crime story, and if you, my dear collaborators, will cast your memories back to A. E. W. Mason's superb *House of the Arrow*, you will remember the horrid thrill it gave one when one realised that it was the young and beautiful heroine who was the guilty one, and when one found that everything fell into place, that the psychology was correct and that nothing had been forced. I admit that if Penelope is the guilty one we are left without love interest (which is not a thing that interests me personally in a detective story). However, I have introduced another girl who will grow on one as the book goes on—it sounds rather like a fungus, but you know what I mean. She is the Paulina Home de Bassompierre to Penelope's Ginevra Fanshawe.

Dr Cheedle being a reputable practitioner, who keeps his poison cupboard locked, Penelope, like the rest of us, can only get hold of arsenic *via* our old friend the weed-killer. She is secretary to Mr Walton, the solicitor; consequently she knows all about his correspondence, and she knows why his son, Dr Walton of Harley Street, is sending that particular nurse. Penelope has some Sleepine cachets prescribed for her by her father when she had influenza, and hence, when the nurse comes to tea that afternoon and complains of a headache, she puts the stuff into the very black strong sweetened tea that Nurse Ponting drinks; she puts the harmless cachet in a box for her, telling her it's one of her father's 'flu cure powders. In this way Penelope is safeguarded, because suppose the nurse doesn't die, but is only made very ill by the over-dose, the other can be analysed and found harmless, and the nurse would simply think she had an idiosyncrasy for the influenza cure.

I see no reason why Dr Cheedle should pretend to John that the nurse hadn't been in his house. It doesn't seem to me quite normal and natural. Surely Nurse Ponting would have been very surprised that there was no one to meet her? Surely Dr Cheedle would have invited her to his house wishing to speak to her about his peculiar patient before she met her? Remember that Dr Cheedle doesn't know that any serious suspicions against anyone are held or the reason for this particular nurse being sent. Anyway, when she's not met, I think it is perfectly natural for her to go straight to Dr Cheedle, and I should have thought that as Dr Cheedle has arranged for John to call in, he would have asked him to take the nurse back to Mrs Farland.

I agree that the difficulty in this is that since the poison is, from my point of view, administered to her by Penelope at Dr Cheedle's, she would die in John's car, which would never do. However, I think this difficulty can be got out of by Penelope telling the nurse that John has made a mistake about the train and is going to meet her at Creepe Station. The nurse, already feeling a little giddy, says she would like the walk back to the station. This doesn't seem to me to present any difficulty.

I see nothing odd in the fact that the nurse finds out that the station-master is a married man. Personally I never seem to have a porter or taxi-driver without getting to know all his affairs. One is like that, or one isn't. In fact, I imagine Miss Sayers means all this station stuff to be a whole shop full of cunning red herrings.

I account for the flask found in the general waiting-room by the fact that Nurse Ponting had already begun to suspect that she was suffering from 'flu and when Dr Walton gave her this job she compromised with her conscience by saying to herself that she would easily cure it by aspirin and rum or brandy, and need not infect her patient. It must be realised that Nurse Ponting is very hard up and desperately anxious not to lose a case. Feeling ill and faint from the Sleepine she has taken in strong sweet tea with Penelope, she drinks a small dose of rum out of the flask—that is if the flask is kept in the story at all. I think it is very important and must be kept in. It would be the chief thing to distract suspicion from the Cheedle household.

I agree with Mr Freeman Wills Crofts and Mr Valentine Williams that the two murders are undoubtedly connected one with the other and that whoever is poisoning Mrs Farland is determined that Nurse Ponting will never live to attend her. That idea of Mr Crofts' that Nurse Ponting has been mixed up in a murder trial before is grand. After all, we must remember that Mrs Farland is being poisoned by arsenic, and even if the poisoner in a fit of fear were to stay his hand the presence of arsenic would be discovered in her hair, her nails, and in her specimens, which this new nurse would take.

I don't see anything unusual in John's insistence on fetching the nurse. What does strike me as unusual is that it was not all cut and dried between him and Dr Cheedle that Nurse Ponting was going to be met. I agree with Miss Sayers that the most likely thing is that Dr Cheedle has asked her to come by an earlier train to take a cup of tea at his house, so that he can tell her about his patient.

Of course, if my solution about Penelope is adopted, John doesn't take Nurse Ponting into the wood, and she quite openly has tea upstairs with Penelope after talking to the doctor.

I think the most important thing in a detective story is that everyone should behave as humanly and as naturally as possible. If (and Dr Cheedle is undoubtedly right) she took an over-dose of Sleepine about half an hour before it took effect, it is obvious that she must be got out of the house by Penelope as quickly as possible, and the time is just nicely covered by walking to the station, where John is going to meet her, drinking her brandy (or her rum) as she feels ill, and passing into a coma. As Miss Sayers points out, the action of barbituric depends on the individual reaction, and the normal thing for the police to think (seeing that there is no concealment about the fact that the nurse has had tea with the Cheedles) is that the nurse took her dose when she drank from the flask at the station.

It is of course obvious to the authors, though I trust it will not be to the readers, that Joan Cliff, feeling sure that her aunt must have been poisoned, comes down to do a little detective work on her own. The only person who suspects this is Penelope, who finally decides she may as well be hanged for three sheep, and goes after Joan and very nearly succeeds in killing her. The unfortunate successor, about the last chapter but one, will have this nice little bit of business to deal with. Anyway, John, who has also begun to suspect, saves Joan, and the business starts to clear up.

I hope there is someone specially engaged to go through all the chapters and see that we have none of us overlooked any contradictory or superfluous facts. This sort of writing is so intensely difficult. For instance, I have had to have the temerity of suggesting to my predecessors that they alter one or two things here and there—so that there must be someone with an all-seeing-eye like that of God.

Those are my only criticisms so far. My predecessors have presented me with a grand lot of characters, all in the round, so I give them my thanks, and to my successor I give my heartfelt sympathies. The unfortunate authors who write the last two chapters should receive some kind of medal.

PART FIVE

by Anthony Armstrong

NOTES

Quite frankly I think this is the most terrible job I've ever had! The ingenuity of my predecessors has left me gasping like a fish out of its element, as indeed I am in this particular type of novel. The story seems to abound with potential murderers, till my brain reels, and I even begin to suspect either Pearn, Pollinger, or Higham, [*Dorothy L. Sayers' literary agents, whose names were stamped on every third or fourth page of her manuscript.*] whose names appear without clues, but with devastating frequency in the earlier part.

Like F.T.J. I very much hope there *is* an ALL-SEEING EYE OF GOD to go through the tale afterwards (and I rather suspect this A.S.E.O.G. might be Miss Sayers), because it must be arranged that our ultimate murderer is not someone into whose obviously innocent thoughts at any material time when he was not in the running, the reader has been allowed to see. I am assuming, therefore, without intending to be officious, that various alterations will be made in our instalments to bring them into line with those of our successors. Anyone is at liberty to alter mine in any way they like.

So to my successor I bequeath these my notes and chapter, and may Gawd have mercy on his soul!

1. I have of course been left with no choice but to continue what F.T.J. has well and rightly started, namely, Billingham's interview of the people in the house. During this, too, suspicion must be kept distributed. The question is: who really *has* done it? Here, while admiring F.T.J.'s brilliant suggestion of Penelope as the only possible person on whom *suspicion doesn't fall*, I cannot quite agree with it. Suspicion *doesn't* fall, largely because in the first place no mention has been made, in its proper place earlier on, of the Nurse having had tea with Penelope; merely that Cheedle showed her out at 3 o.c., while Penelope has never even met her. This will, of course, have to be altered as F.T.J. suggests in her notes; but I submit that if various facts, namely, that Sleepine caused death, that it could have been administered in strong tea, that it was administered at 3.30, and that Penelope had tea alone with the victim at that time, are all brought out together, as they would naturally have been, it will be very difficult to avoid *some* suspicion falling on Penelope.

Again, another reason why we haven't suspected her up to now is that her actions—the hearing of the footsteps and the shutting door, etc.—are described by V.W. from her (Penelope's) point of view, which appears to be that of an *innocent* person. And even supposing we *do* make her the murderess, I do not think she ought to try to kill Joan Cliff as well. She can't go *on* in her impulsive, girlish manner bumping off everybody who looked like finding her out; or it'll become more of a profession than a hobby. For these reasons I am against Penelope as the guilty one.

But I do think F.T.J.'s suggestion is too good to be wasted, and so would like to have her (Penelope, of course, not F.T.J.) falsely suspected for most of my chapter, so as to try and get a little of the *House of the Arrow* thrill in. In this connection would A.S.E.O.G. (when re-doing that earlier part as it will have to be done) be so kind as to let Penelope, the Nurse *and* Cheedle be reported to have all had tea together that Sunday afternoon, instead of Penelope and Nurse only, and also try to avert the suspicion that either might have put the stuff in her cup—by perhaps giving an opportunity elsewhere for someone else to have done it, or for her to have taken it herself? And would A.S.E.O.G. also deal

129

with the question of Penelope's hearing someone in the dressing-room, then hearing steps going downstairs, and yet making no mention of this very suspicious point to Billingham? Could it not be the old lady who thinks she heard the noise and sends her to investigate, and could not Penelope then hear something in there, but not be certain? Thus Penelope would not think it very important and might forget to mention it to Billingham. She might recollect it later on, in my successor's chapter—perhaps giving him a needed clue?

2. I personally am inclined to plump for a guilty false-hero John Farland, suggested by F.W.C. and cleverly followed up by V.W. in his notes (the ones of Parry's motor-bike, etc.) as far as *Mrs Farland's* murder is concerned; and I also agree with his note 11, that the police will assume the same person did both murders. *But* I think that is a grand *false* assumption for them, and the reader, to make; and so I would not have Farland do the Ponting murder as well! After all, as F.T.J. says, the 'nasty cold drink in the nasty cold wood' theory of F.W.C. *is* hard to swallow. However deserted Creepe may be on wet Sundays, it only needs (over a longish period) just *one* person to see him, a well-known local figure, in the company of the subsequently murdered nurse in her

conspicuous uniform and his guilt will stand out a mile. He'd *never* risk it!

I therefore suggest Dr Cheedle as the actual murderer of Nurse Ponting. He had guessed some while ago what John Farland was up to, but he has said nothing; hinting, however, to Farland that he'll keep his eyes shut if he is given a 'cut', *his* motive being money troubles. This will also help to explain a point which has apparently not worried my predecessors but has worried me a whole lot. If Cheedle is *innocent*, why has he not, when confronted with a woman who insists she is being poisoned,—so much so that a nurse experienced in such cases, is sent for,—taken the normal medical steps to investigate the possibility of, at any rate, arsenic? My Encyclopaedia informs me that the similarity of the symptoms of arsenic poisoning to 'those of cholera, is very marked, but *if the suspicion arises* it can soon be cleared up by examining any of the secretions'. A doctor also tells me that any G.P. under similar circumstances would, unless he were either guilty or a complete damfool, almost certainly have taken some steps to rule out the arsenic possibilities by sending samples away for a Rheinsch or, more likely, Marsh test (as in the Armstrong poisoning case—no relation, I hasten to add!) The answer, to my mind, is that

Cheedle is a sleeping partner in the crime, and when the nurse appears and he knows the game will be up, he takes a more active part by removing *her*. He was, of course, prepared to give a death certificate for Mrs Farland, but Parry was there *first!* In fact, I rather like the whole idea!

So to help this, would A.S.E.O.G. consider keeping out the earlier specific references to arsenic? It tends to throw suspicion on Cheedle for not doing anything about it, and moreover it is quite a point to let the death by *arsenic*, when she has been taking Sleepine, which has already killed one person, come as a surprise.

3. As, I understand, there is only one more unfortunate conspirator to follow me and finish, I shall have to get on fairly quickly with the story and shall take it on, after the false Penelope trail, as far as a very definite implication of Cheedle for my 'curtain'. I hope this won't tie my successor's hand too much, but it will give him the chance to let the police then work on their natural assumption that the same hand must have done Mrs Farland in too, so he can spring a good surprise with John Farland. (Or with anyone else?) The mud on the motor-bike, the shortage of petrol, Penelope's hearing footsteps, will all help, and I shouldn't be surprised if J.F. had been called on for a song or speech at the concert between 9.30

and 10—and couldn't be found. I think there might be a good 'dust up' between Farland and Cheedle at the end. Penelope, of course, can be paired off with Parry.

Well, anyhow, to get on with the story as I see it—

I

Inspector Billingham wasn't himself when Dr Cheedle came into the room. He was agitated and unhappy. He loathed to think that Penelope might be guilty, but all the time she was becoming more horribly suspect.

'I've just had your daughter in here, sir,' he said, as soon as the little doctor was seated in front of him the other side of the desk. 'What she told me points to a serious discrepancy in your earlier statements.'

Cheedle's eyes seemed to flicker. He opened his mouth, shut it again, looked down at the floor, then said:

'Well, what did she tell you?'

'That she was in your house when Nurse Ponting called on Sunday.'

Cheedle nodded placidly.

'That's quite true. I deceived you about it, not because I wanted to impede you in any way, but because Penelope and I had our reasons for pretending she was out, and it didn't seem to have any bearing on the matter anyhow.'

'I see,' said Billingham. 'Well, I'd like you to tell me exactly what did happen in your house on Sunday afternoon.'

Cheedle cleared his throat.

'To begin with, I knew that Nurse Ponting was coming on the early train, because I telegraphed her to do so.'

'You did, did you!'

'I wanted a few minutes' chat with her before she came here to Whitestones, and I didn't want any of the suspects to know that I had seen her. Unfortunately, Penelope had made an arrangement to meet John Farland at my house at the same hour that I was expecting the nurse. Though I have never for a moment believed he could be guilty, he is undoubtedly a suspect, and I didn't want him there with Nurse Ponting.'

'Well?' said Billingham.

'It was difficult to give Penelope a plausible reason for not keeping her arrangement with Farland. She isn't the sort of girl who can be easily taken in. I had to confide in her, and she was naturally furious and horrified to discover that I classed her fiancé amongst the suspects.'

He smiled rather bleakly.

'I pointed out to her,' he said, 'that she, too, had a reason for wanting Mrs Farland out of the way, and that made her angrier still. But in the end she calmed down, and consented to allowing me to lie to Farland when he called. But she made me promise never to let anybody know that she had really been in the house all the time, in case he should find out.'

It sounded reasonable, Billingham thought, and he felt a little happier about Penelope. At any rate Cheedle's story fitted hers in every particular. He began questioning Cheedle about Mrs Farland's death, but on that point the doctor hadn't much to say. In the first place he had only arrived after Mrs Farland had died, and secondly he was unwilling to give any opinion as to the cause of death until, if possible, after the post-mortem, and at any rate after he had consulted with Dr Parry, who had been present at the actual death. The latter had been called away on an urgent case soon after his partner's arrival—for the business of being born, dying, being ill, and getting well again still went on in Creepe, and Mrs Farland would never again have a use for two doctors at once at her bedside. Besides, as Billingham could see, Cheedle was absolutely fagged out, and even inclined to be snappy.

'The post-mortem,' he said with finality, 'will tell us definitely what we want to know; till then, Inspector, I don't honestly see I can do much good by making guesses.'

'Quite—quite,' said Billingham reserving to himself the thought that most of a doctor's

135

business seemed to be guess-work anyway. 'By the way, about that Sleepine bottle: would you have any means of knowing whether it had been changed, as Dr Parry suggested?'

'I would,' replied Cheedle grimly. 'Because if the result of the analysis of the cachets which you're having made now shows any tampering with the Sleepine content, then obviously it's not the bottle I left out.'

'Naturally ... Well, I don't think I'll trouble you further for the moment. It's a pretty queer business altogether.'

'It is. Very. And I can repeat, Inspector, what I indicated to you over the 'phone last night: that in my opinion and in Dr Parry's, my patient did not die a natural death. I'll even go a step further. I'll add that I'm equally certain that she did not kill herself.'

'Leaving murder, eh?' said Billingham.

'Leaving murder,' repeated Dr Cheedle, and rose to go.

Billingham sat down to think. His mind, in an effort to absolve Penelope, suddenly flashed back momentarily to the empty whisky flask found in the waiting-room by Tom Tadman. Was it Nurse Ponting's? If so, she must have brought it with her: it couldn't have been purchased in Creepe, for all the pubs were shut. Or had it been given her by someone that afternoon? He had naturally had a man going round the inns and grocers, to see if he could find out who had bought a similar bottle in the last two days, but he didn't expect this would lead to anything positive. Anyway, one thing was certain, and that was that Nurse Ponting's death was connected with that of Mrs Farland. It made him feel guilty to remember his interview with her yesterday. She had guessed that she hadn't much longer to live. But what could he have done about it, anyway?

He had read about or followed all the big murder trials of the last fifty years, and he knew well how often the old phrase 'cui bono' was justified. Ninety-nine murders out of a hundred-excluding those committed for revenge or by sex-maniacs—were undertaken to remove someone who stood between the murderer and something he wanted, whether money, freedom, secrecy, a loved one, and so on. And to whose advantage in Creepe and the neighbourhood had it been to remove Nurse Ponting? Obviously it was the person who was trying to remove Mrs Farland-just as she had told him yesterday—and who, wishing naturally that his endeavours should not come to light, feared that Nurse Ponting's appearance would upset his apple-cart. Billingham was willing at that moment to bet a hundred quid that the two murders were committed by the same hand. And that—regrettable though the second murder was—certainly tended to make his task easier because, assuming a murderer has, say, but one chance in five of getting away, he has only one in twenty-five, if he is forced, or is foolish enough, to commit another. The odds are multiplied, not merely added.

To whose advantage then, real or presumed—for even murderers make unfortunate errors—had it been to remove Mrs Farland? A clue to that, thought Billingham, would soon be given by the contents of the will. One of the people suspected must be due to come into a bit, and it would be very interesting to know just who. Not that he would be foolish enough to let himself be unjustifiably biased by the knowledge, but—well, he always had great faith in what he called 'Good old Kwy Bonno' as a pointer.

At this juncture John Farland came into the room, and soon after he had briefly confirmed his movements of the previous night, the Inspector suddenly found himself with one of the pointers he had been looking for.

'You mustn't mind these questions,' he had said kindly, 'but this affair is really very serious.'

'I'm inclined to agree with you now,' returned the young man gravely. 'And to my mind one of the horrible things about it is that we never really took my aunt seriously. Dr Parry, you know, was convinced that her accusations were hysteria—and now it looks as though they were true all the time. We even joked about it. Why, I remember on the very afternoon we got that poor nurse down, just in case there *was* any truth in ...' He broke off suddenly.

'Well, sir?' said Billingham. 'What's the matter?'

'Nothing. I just realised that all this hasn't anything much to do with it.'

'In a case like this everything helps.'

'Well, I was only going to say I actually ragged Millie, Miss Pink that is, about it being her last chance to finish the old lady off. Rather terrible, wasn't it; but I might just as well have made the joke about myself. I was quite often one of the suspects.'

Billingham nodded, and remembered the window in John Farland's sitting-room. It would have been very easy for him to have left the house unseen on Sunday afternoon and met Nurse Ponting somewhere.

'You were, of course, suspected as your aunt's nearest relative and presumably her heir?' he threw out skilfully.

'I suppose so. Not that she could do very much about it. In fact, it really rather annoyed her that I was the one person she couldn't threaten to cut off with a shilling if she wanted to. I get £15,000 anyway from my late uncle.'

Ah, thought the Inspector to himself at this point, there's one Kwy Bonno anyway. Aloud he said: 'But that wasn't all she had?'

'Oh, no. There's quite a bit more. I believe I was in the running for it at one time. But lately she's been using the promise of it—well, quite frankly, as a sort of sword over Miss Pink's head, to secure all the slavish attention she could. You know! The last week or so, for instance, Millie's been in favour, but by tomorrow she'd have been right out of the will. Following week back again probably . . .'

'Then Miss Pink was due to be cut out again?' asked Billingham, studying his finger-nails.

John Farland paused a moment with wrinkled forehead.

'Since you ask me, as far as I know—yes. But'—he suddenly became a little heated—'that's a terribly awkward question for me to answer. I very nearly said I didn't really know.'

'Why, sir?' asked Billingham smoothly. He seemed to be getting somewhere: another Kwy Bonno already! 'It never pays to lie to the police.'

'Yes, I know.'

'Why, then?'

'For two reasons. First of all, I'm not supposed to know about it. Miss Cheedle told me last night, and she shouldn't have done—she's a confidential secretary. I suppose she thought a fiancé was privileged.'

'Right, I'll forget that,' lied the Inspector, storing up in his mind the fact that here at any rate were two people who had known where the bulk of the old lady's money was to go. 'And what was your second reason?' he asked.

'Well...' John Farland again hesitated. 'I suddenly realised that telling you that would make things look a little black for poor Millie. Not that she'd have the courage to hurt a fly, but still the inference...' He broke off, obviously ill at ease, then burst out with apparent sincerity: 'You can take it from me, Millie *couldn't* have done such a thing. She had a rotten time of it with Aunt Emma—her life was rather hell, you know, but she was really a born slave, and as far as...'

'Oh, we mustn't think things like that,' put in Billingham, adding, 'yet' to himself. 'Then is there anything more you can tell me? Any fact that might have some bearing on this unfortunate business?'

'Nothing, I'm afraid.' John Farland smiled frankly. 'Still, somebody must have done it—and I suppose we're all suspect?'

The Inspector rose. 'As you say, sir, someone must have done it.' He did not, however, repeat the rest of the sentence. 'Well, I'll see Miss Pink now,' he finished, and opened the door.

'I'll tell her,' replied John Farland and went.

Billingham stood for a moment looking at the door through which John Farland had gone. In reality he was trying to look beyond the door to the young man himself and even further, into

141

his soul. Was he just what he seemed—amiable, easy-going, not too fond of his aunt, and yet not hypocritical enough to pretend a sorrow he didn't feel? Or was he a clever, cold-blooded murderer, who had put two people out of the way, just because he couldn't hang on for a few more years for his £15,000? Of course with a beauty like Penelope waiting to become his very own, as soon as he could afford marriage, a different complexion was put on the matter.

'I wonder,' said Billingham aloud and sat down to wait for Miss Pink, Miss Pink, who, if John Farland was speaking the truth, was to have been cut out of the will this very day.

But it was not after all Millie who in a moment tapped at the door and entered.

It was Joan Cliff, and a few minutes later, looking rather like a pretty little brown mouse, she was sitting in the big chair talking earnestly to an attentive Billingham.

'I hoped you wouldn't mind,' she said; 'but I felt I had to see you as soon as possible, and Miss Pink is still in a terrible state of tears and nerves and goodness knows what.' She paused. 'It's about my aunt; she was Nurse Ponting, you know?'

'I know. Miss Cheedle told me who you were.'

'I—I was very fond of Aunt Hilda.' Her lovely eyes filled a little and Billingham looked awkwardly away. 'I don't know what the

Inquest will say—but I *know* she didn't die naturally.'

'I agree with you, Miss Cliff. I'm sorry to say my opinion is that she was murdered.'

He was liking this small, direct young person very much, and felt that he needn't bother to mince words.

'Yes. So I thought if I could be of any help ... For instance, I brought this...' She started to fumble in her bag. 'I didn't see any mention of it in any of the papers, only something about Aunt Hilda having come by mistake on a train that got in too early, when that was only an *excuse*. I know because we invented it together beforehand.' She handed a crumpled sheet of paper to Billingham, who smoothed it out.

'Oh, Dr Cheedle's telegram!'

'Then you know?'

'Well, only recently,' explained Billingham, looking at the wire, which ran much as he had expected: '*Would like to see you quite privately before proceeding Yowle case. Suggest you catch 1.31 Paddington instead of train arranged. Come my house Creepe afternoon.*' It was signed 'Dr Cheedle.'

'Hm,' grunted Billingham. 'He's spent a bit of money on it.'

'I don't see how he could have put it shorter,' objected Joan. 'You see, *he* didn't know my aunt at all. As a matter of fact she was expecting some suggestion of the sort—in view of the

143

particular case . . .'

'Yes, that's right,' said Billingham. He had overlooked the point.

'We talked it over—Aunt Hilda was really rather unhappy about the whole thing—and we made up the story . . . But,' she broke off . . . 'I'm sorry to have bothered you, seeing you know all about it.'

'Quite all right, Miss Cliff.'

She suddenly appeared more nervous. 'Then may I bother you again—about this last—death?'

'That's what I'm here for,' smiled the other. 'Nothing's unimportant.'

'Miss Pink didn't come downstairs till after Miss Cheedle and her father had left, and while you were talking to Mr Farland, so I introduced myself and we got talking together. She was telling me all about last night, describing what happened . . .'

'Go on,' prompted Billingham kindly.

'Well—the symptoms at the end—they were'—she blurted it out with a rush—'absolutely those of arsenic poisoning.'

'Arsenic!' Billingham whistled.

'The Heaviside case was arsenic, you know, and I know a lot about it from my aunt. They're very distinctive symptoms—burning in the stomach and nausea, cramp in the calves—and other things . . . of course, this is only guesswork.'

144

'I shall know any minute. I'm expecting an analysis. But I confess I hadn't thought of arsenic. My mind was on this infernal Sleepine. It was that which was responsible for your aunt's death, and the same stuff was being taken in this case.'

He appeared sunk in thought and Joan Cliff got up. 'If there's anything else I can tell you, I'll be only too glad. I'm up for the Inquest, and shall have to stay on for—for the funeral arrangements.'

'Good! Then maybe I'll get in touch with you later. Oh, by the way,' he added, as she was going. 'You can tell me one thing now. Did your aunt ever drink whisky at any time, and if so, what brand? Black Horse, for instance?'

The girl smiled faintly. 'No, she was a rabid teetotaller. Unfortunately—because I'm not.'

'Thanks,' said Billingham thoughtfully.

The girl left and the Inspector once more wandered across to the window. Arsenic, by Jove! It was quite a probability. This Joan Cliff seemed to know what she was talking about. And if it *was* arsenic then at any rate that seemed to rule out either of the doctors as having had a hand in the old lady's death, for surely with all resources of the pharmacopoeia at his disposal a medical man would hardly choose arsenic as his weapon; arsenic, the one poison that literally could rise from the grave years after and jerk a murderer out of his fool's paradise of fancied security straight to the foot of the gallows.

The telephone in the corner suddenly rang and a voice asked for him. It was the call he had been expecting.

The analyst was able to assure him that there was no trace of arsenic in any of the cachets remaining in the new bottle. They contained Sleepine and nothing else!

At that moment Millie Pink came into the room.

II

Millie had recovered herself somewhat, though her unattractive appearance had certainly not been improved by the constant bouts of weeping in which she had been indulging. But at least they had had this effect: she had cried so much she couldn't at the moment cry any more. Thus the Inspector was at least able to get a fairly coherent story, and since Millie was apparently nothing if not observant, a useful one.

She told how she had been given the new bottle by Penelope, had put it by the side of the other in the dressing-room cupboard and was tidying the cupboard, when she had been rather abruptly sent to bed. She went on to talk about her subsequent meeting with Penelope, saying that she had heard her name mentioned by Mrs Farland and frankly had stopped to listen.

'Eavesdropping, I suppose it'd be called,' she confessed with a simper.

'But why?'

'Because Mrs Farland had been rather beastly to me that evening, and Mr Walton was coming to see her today, and I—I wondered if she was going to take me out of her will again and was telling Miss Cheedle about it.'

'Was she?'

'I—I don't know,' faltered Millie. 'I didn't hear anything and Penelope wouldn't tell me afterwards.'

'Anyway,' smiled Billingham with assumed carelessness, 'it makes no difference now, does it? I mean, it's too late.'

Watching her keenly, he saw her plain face light up with a sudden irradiation of happiness that was a revelation to him.

'I—I never thought of that. All this business ... Why, I ...' To Billingham's amazement she burst into a flood of tears for about the tenth time that morning.

Feeling he could get no more out of her, he let her go and paid a brief visit to the room upstairs. This told him nothing; as Cheedle had said, the post-mortem was the only thing that would help. Then he left Whitestones and clattered off in the Ford to Creepe.

At the Creepe Station he phoned his chief a

report of the affair and his investigations to date. He also asked permission, in view of this new complication, to request the Coroner to adjourn that day's Inquest on Nurse Ponting pending further police inquiries. Then he went off to Mr Walton's office to 'check up', as he put it, on 'his two Kwy Bonnos'.

Here after a long battle of words with the crusty Mr Walton, who had all the lawyer's secretiveness, and thought the police might just as well wait till the will was made public, he managed to extract confirmation of John Farland's fifteen thousand pounds' interest, and of the fact that, after allowing for various small legacies to minor favourites of the moment, Millie Pink came into the remainder, which would be about twenty-five thousand pounds. He also learnt, after more argument, that John Farland's other statement had been correct; Mrs Farland was intending that day to remake her will and cut Millie Pink out of it altogether.

'In favour of whom?'

'That at any rate hardly applies now,' said Walton stiffly.

'Still, I'd like to know, sir, *if* you don't mind.'

'And I say, *if* you don't mind, that it can have no possible bearing on the unfortunate occurrence, and would be mere wanton violation of my dead client's confidence.'

Billingham, trying to control his temper,

argued further, but the other was adamant, and as it was then nearly the hour set for the Inquest, he had to go.

The Inquest did not take very long. The finding of the body and the cause of death were formally proved—and then the Coroner announced that at police request the proceedings would be adjourned for eight days.

Inspector Billingham thereupon retired to a quiet corner of the Eagle coffee-room for a well-earned chop and a lot of hard thinking. A good solid reasoning out of facts generally got him somewhere, and he always found he could think very well while eating. Probably—as his wife used to suggest—the rhythmical movement of the jaws helped, for she declared she never knew a man who could chew a mouthful so long and still swallow it at the end!

From the shelves of his mind he selected the bottle of cachets to work upon and started off, busily champing and thinking. Although the analyst had not discovered arsenic in the cachets that remained, it was still possible that the cachets given to Mrs Farland had contained that poison.

But even apart from the fact, he argued to himself, that if Dr Cheedle had wanted to poison his own patient, he almost certainly wouldn't have used arsenic, it further seemed highly unlikely that he would have deliberately made the pills up and left them for another

149

doctor to take over, and for others to discover later. Far too risky. It looked, therefore, very much as if the fatal bottle had been substituted *after* he had put it out. Now it was also highly unlikely, thought Billingham, that this had been done by Parry, because he himself had called attention to the fact that it had been changed. Unless, of course, he had said that as a clever blind, but then Parry, too, would scarcely have used arsenic. At the moment the weight of probability was that the bottle had been changed sometime after Parry had handed it to Penelope Cheedle—who had taken it upstairs and given it to Millie Pink to put in the cupboard . . .

At this point Billingham gave a sudden exclamation, swallowed a bit of potato the wrong way, and wasn't himself for some minutes, besides attracting a good deal of amused attention in the coffee-room. The cause of all this was that he had just remembered that Penelope Cheedle had said, and repeated it later, that Dr Parry was entirely wrong in saying it wasn't the same Sleepine bottle. There was something queer there: it hadn't been at all a natural thing to say. For if (argued Billingham to the accompaniment of chop) someone remarks to you, 'I remember noticing a nick on the bottle I brought out, and this one hasn't got one, therefore they are not the same,' you simply cannot with any logicality assert that he

150

is mistaken, and that he was tired and it was late—assert, in fact, that he imagined noticing a nick! A statement of that nature could only be made if the thing were the other way round, if he had remarked to you: 'The bottle I brought out had no nick on it and this one has.' You might then suggest he had failed to notice the nick, which had been there all the time. Yes, thought Billingham rather excitedly, if Parry said he noticed a nick, either he was lying, in which case it was a deliberate attempt to pretend the bottle had been changed; or else there *had* been a nick there, in which case Penelope Cheedle had no earthly basis in reason for asserting so definitely he was wrong. *Unless*—and Billingham's jaws actually stopped working in his excitement—she had wanted to pretend the bottle hadn't been changed, and . . . Good Lord, thought Billingham, perhaps she had changed it *herself* . . .

For a moment he felt quite a shock at finding his suspicions thus suddenly directed again upon such a beautiful creature as Penelope. Then he realized rather wretchedly that one's outside appearance does not reflect the soul inside. Attracted though he naturally might be by the girl, he was a policeman with a job to be done, and Penelope, as John Farland's fiancée, was also a 'Kwy Bonno'.

He swallowed his long overdue mouthful and started eating and thinking again on this line, to realize reluctantly that things seemed to fit in only too well. For Penelope would be quite likely to use arsenic, one of the few poisons open to her to obtain without much suspicion; Penelope had plenty of opportunities of getting at and doctoring the cachets her father was taking over; Penelope, too, had, so Parry had told him, actually met him alone downstairs and taken the new bottle from him. Terrible as it was, everything seemed to point to Penelope Cheedle.

At this point Billingham mopped his forehead, took a large draught of beer, and switching from chop to Cheddar cheese, switched at the same time to Nurse Ponting's death, for the two were so obviously by the same hand.

And here again, like a blow in the face, came further implication of Penelope. She had had tea alone with the nurse, just about the time that on the doctor's reckoning the Sleepine must have been administered. She knew what the nurse had come for, and she realized the game would probably soon be up. She had no doubt instigated her father to send that telegram; and she had Sleepine actually in her possession for her 'flu.

'My God!' thought Billingham to himself; 'Supposing this is all true, that girl could yet sit there this morning, looking straight at me with those lovely blue eyes.'

What was it she had said, too, about Sleepine: 'You always hear of a thing three times. Nurse Ponting who took it, and me and Mrs Farland...' His quick brain suddenly seized on another small point; the girl had mentioned Sleepine in connection with Mrs Farland, when it was arsenic that had killed her. Of course that was just the assumption an innocent person might make. But it was also just the point a guilty person would bring in to prove they didn't know it was arsenic.

With his head in a considerable whirl, he got up hurriedly and left. He had to see Penelope Cheedle again and soon...

Outside in the street he nearly found himself threatened with the police by an irate waiter, who had to run after him with his bill.

III

'Walton & Bloomfield, the lawyers, were on the phone for you, sir, a while back,' announced Sergeant Craven. The Inspector had stopped in at the station on his way to see if any messages had come for him. 'Wouldn't say what it was.'

'Right! Get them for me, will you,' and Billingham sat down to wait.

Sitting there he pondered a new aspect of the case. If Penelope Cheedle *had* changed the bottles, why on earth hadn't she changed them back, and so averted suspicion. She had had, as far as he could make out, ample opportunities for so doing while Mrs Farland was in that last fatal coma, for John Farland was telephoning the doctor, the maid filling the hot-water bottle; there was only Millie's presence to reckon with, and she would be in such a fluster she'd never notice anything. His instinctive male sympathy for the lovely girl was now warring with his instinctive desire to lay the murderer by the heels, and he almost hoped that this new line might lead away from Penelope. But after a moment's reasoning he sadly shook his head.

The girl knew well enough, as he had learnt from John Farland, that Millie was to be cut out of the will next day. *Not* to change the bottles again would be a good move on her part; for it would undoubtedly throw suspicion on Millie Pink. This also seemed to clear Millie Pink, he thought; for she most certainly would have changed the bottles back had she been guilty; unless, as was remotely possible, she was in too much of a fluster at the actual death really occurring at last.

'Mr Walton's not back from lunch yet, sir,' called Craven from the 'phone. He put his hand over the mouthpiece. 'Nearly three, too. You'd think all that eating'd put some flesh on the old broomstick, but it don't!' And Craven, his best, and usually sole—audience, laughed heartily.

'Tell him to ring me here. I'll wait,' said

Billingham. Then he sighed. It looked very like Penelope. Of course, not changing those darn bottles back to throw suspicion elsewhere would apply just as well to John Farland, but then he'd been at the smoking concert all evening till past eleven and so couldn't have made the substitution in the first place.

'Gawd, what a mix-up!' said Billingham aloud and had an idea. 'Craven!' he called. 'I've got a job for a smart young constable—say Bratton.'

'What's he to do, sir?'

'Somewhere over at Whitestones I suspect there's a bottle of Sleepine cachets, probably unopened.'

'Lumme, that stuff again!'

'Yes. This is the bottle that Mrs Farland should have had and it'll have a nick in the inside of the lip. I'm assuming the murderer took steps to dispose of it as soon as possible, in case he was found with it. Try the dustbin—though it won't be there—any pond, well, crevices in walls, disused ditches—you get the idea—where someone might have slipped out and hidden it that night. Try inside too—though it won't be there either. In fact I don't think he'll find it at all. But if he does he'll have done a good job. A nick inside the neck, remember.'

'I'll tell him, sir,' said Craven, much impressed by what appeared to him sheer

155

Sherlock Holmes stuff, and just then the telephone rang.

'Inspector Billingham?' It was Walton's curt, crisp voice. 'Since our interview this morning I have talked things over with my partner. He is of the opinion that I was wrong to refuse you any information, however irrelevant, under the circumstances obtaining.'

'Thank you, sir,' the Inspector glued his ear firmly to the phone. What was coming now, he asked himself?

'Mrs Farland's intention in omitting Miss Pink from her will, was to replace her by Miss Penelope Cheedle.'

'Good G ... I mean, is that so?'

'I've told you!' snapped the solicitor.

'But ... yes ... one minute, Mr Walton!' Billingham's mind was working fast. He realized at once that the case against Penelope was badly damaged by this, for who would kill anyone the day *before* she was going to be made heir to twelve thousand.

'I'm waiting,' came Walton's voice.

'Sorry! What I'd like to know is this: Did Miss Cheedle, as your secretary, know of this?'

'Naturally not. Mrs Farland mentioned it to me personally and I have told no one, certainly not Miss Cheedle. Good afternoon!'

Billingham turned away and lit a cigarette. He wondered whether Mrs Farland might not have told the girl herself that last night. Only

156

two people would know that—and one was
dead, while the other, if guilty, would probably
lie. He went out into the street. It was more
than ever imperative that he should see
Penelope Cheedle again.

IV

But a strange thing happened on the way. On
the street ahead of him he saw Dr Cheedle and
hurrying after him, he tapped him on the arm.
To his amazement the little doctor jumped
violently and dropped some letters he was
taking to the post.

'Stupid of me!' he apologized. 'My nerves are
in a bad way after the last few days.'

'Stupid of *me*!' countered Billingham, helping
him pick up the letters.

But he did not after all ask the doctor the
questions he had intended, and after chatting a
few minutes, let the other go on his way. For
his own part he turned back to the station and
put through a call to a certain London police
headquarters. For he had seen the address on
one of the letters, and it was that of a
well-known firm of money-lenders. He felt, in
his own words, he'd know more about Cheedle
when he knew more about his home-life, and
this looked like an opportunity.

Within an hour, with the unofficial help of a

friend in one of the Metropolitan Police Divisions, he had learnt that Dr Cheedle owed the firm of Solomon Mactavish £2,000, and that only last week he had written to say he hoped shortly to be in a position to repay them.

'Whew!' whistled Billingham, as he rang off. For Dr Cheedle was also a 'Kwy Bonno' in some measure, via his daughter and John Farland. And, had it not been rather funny that, with a patient insisting she was being poisoned, so much so that her solicitor actually sent for a nurse experienced in one fatal arsenic case, with all her symptoms pointing as they must have done to arsenic, her doctor should apparently never have let the suspicion enter his head, and should never once have suggested making the simple medical test that would have brought the truth to light?

SUBSEQUENT ROUGH NOTES TO MY SUCCESSOR AFTER READING MY INSTALMENT

Reference my
page 136 Cheedle makes a point of insisting on its being a murder so that the police will presuppose he is not connected with the crime; for he knows that it'll come out anyway at the Inquest. He also tells them about the telegram, which he *had* hoped might never come

up. But the sudden appearance of Joan Cliff forces his hand and so to avoid suspicion he gets it in first. You may want to use these points.

139 I have let Farland make a slip which might be of value to you. Trying to hint that he was one of those who sent for the nurse, he forgot that he was not supposed to have known at the time *why* she was being sent for. (Cheedle of course had passed the information on, which he normally would not have done.) Farland breaks off on realizing what he has done, but quickly covers it.

Farland's earlier mention of Parry here is in *case* you want to make Parry the murderer. He was ostensibly unconnected with the case, and insisted it was mysterious. He also insisted the bottle had been changed. Qy.: to divert suspicion from himself?

140 Farland, having left the bottles unchanged to implicate Millie, is now making certain the Inspector shall suspect her as soon as possible. But—

140 He distracts attention from his action by pretended solicitude for Penelope's breach of confidence: and later by a really genuine outburst in Millie's

favour—genuine enough as he well knows.

143 Joan Cliff, not needed now for love interest, is very useful for having forced Cheedle's hand in re telegram, and also for giving us the first (I hope) arsenic suspicion. She'd come for the Inquest anyway.

145 I have brought in a mention of the empty whisky flask earlier, as F.T.J. advises, and now hint at the fact here that the Nurse could not have drunk from it. This may be of help later on, perhaps to prove that Sleepine was taken in the tea.

146 I have tried to treat the Millie interview in such a way that you may make her guilty, after all, for she had all the opportunity in the world: For, if innocent, wouldn't she really have been hugging herself secretly at the thought of her luck in thus just getting the money, instead of showing she's only just realized? Inference: that it's clever pretence. On the other hand, it'd be very like the flustered Millie not to think of it at all till it was pointed out.

148 Please make any alterations you like to the contents of the will to suit your development. It might well be that John was getting a good bit more on

top of his £15,000, which he would have lost next day; but that Walton says this extra legacy had to be kept an absolute secret from him—one of the old lady's 'surprises?' Somehow or other he had found this out—via Cheedle from Penelope?

150 Penelope's illogical statement *is* rather hard to explain—and frankly it still seems peculiar to me—but you may well like to bring out later that she thought Parry had made some terrible muddle and was trying to protect him, because she really loved him still. This would also prepare for the love-interest when John has been swung off.

155 I have brought in this scene in case later on you want to use as a clue the finding of the original innocent bottle for which the murderer substituted the poison one. This scene can be cut out if not needed.

156 It is still quite open for you to show later that Penelope definitely *did* know she would come into the money, and thus help prove her innocence. Personally, I think Penelope must be out of it now as a suspect and, though I am in favour of John, I hope I have still left you a good choice for the Mrs

Farland murder—Parry, John, Cheedle, Millie—not forgetting Pearn, Pollinger and Higham, Uncle Tom Cobley and all.

PART SIX

by David Hume

I

Inspector Billingham entered the tiny police station to find that Joan Cliff was waiting to see him. The girl's face was flushed, her eyes vividly alive. She hastened to meet the Inspector and together they retired to an inner room.

'And what's the great news, Miss Cliff?' he asked. 'Something exciting?'

'Depends on your point of view,' she replied. 'I was leaving the house to walk into Yowle when I met Millie Pink in the hall. She had a letter in her hand and was complaining how muddy the road was between Whitestones and the pillar-box. I said I'd post the letter for her, and I had the impression that she would rather have posted it herself. Anyway, she gave it to me, and as I walked along the road I examined the envelope—just the ordinary feminine curiosity, I suppose. I'm afraid you'll think I'm a most dreadful person, but Miss Pink's rather mysterious manner about the letter had aroused my curiosity, and I started examining the address. It surprised me, Inspector, that Miss

163

Pink was writing to a man. Didn't seem like her at all. His name is James Wheeler, and he lives at Fasterly. That's about twelve miles from here, isn't it?'

'Yes. But I can't see anything unusual about this, Miss Cliff.'

'You haven't heard the story yet, Inspector. At the finish I did a most dreadful thing. I opened the letter.'

'What on earth made you do a thing like that? It's very, very serious.'

'I just had one of those hunches that we women get occasionally. At any rate I read the letter. Then I came along here immediately. Here it is.'

Joan handed over a mauve envelope. Billingham extracted the double sheet of notepaper, noted the neat, compact hand, the rigid straightness of the lines and commenced to read:

DEAREST,

Within forty-eight hours I will again know the joy of being in your arms. Life for me would be empty indeed if I could not live in the anticipation of your embraces, the rapture of their fulfilment. It seems, beloved, that time stands still when I am locked in your arms, that all things upon this tiresome earth fade away into nothingness.

Since last we were together many

164

unpleasant things have happened, but the recollection of these events will fade beneath the pressure of your caress, the soothing words from your mouth, the glimmer of lovelight in your adorable eyes.

We will meet in the usual place at five o'clock on Friday, my darling. Until then I must wait hungrily for the hours to walk on leaden feet.

My love is entirely yours, dearest.

MILLIE.

Inspector Billingham flushed, stared at Joan Cliff with some show of embarrassment, and laid the letter on the desk. The girl waited for him to speak. Her clearly defined lips twisted in a half-smile.

'An extraordinarily affectionate letter,' said Billingham. 'Miss Pink must have been taking a correspondence course. But why all the air of excitement? Seems like a sickening love parade to me.'

Joan Cliff elevated her eyebrows, or rather the pencilled imitations, and stared at the Inspector with amusement twinkling in her eyes.

'You mean to tell me, Inspector, that the letter conveys nothing to you?'

'It indicates to me that Millie Pink is sex starved, and finds an outlet in her correspondence. Her style is cloying, too flamboyant, very sickly. Is there anything else I'm supposed to deduce from the letter?'

'I'll say there is. You've deduced everything Inspector, except the only thing that matters. Take another look at the letter, and think for a while.'

Billingham read through the letter again, and then shook his head.

'I'll assist you a little,' said Joan. 'You've got a good idea of Millie Pink as you know her. You recall her untidiness, her air of confusion, her attacks of sobbing, her inferiority complex, her constant attacks of semi-hysteria, her awful taste in dress, her almost childish attacks of temper. Remember them?'

'Certainly, I do. What's that got to do with this letter?'

'Just this.' Joan Cliff lowered her voice, bent over the desk, and rapped her fingers on the woodwork to accentuate her words: 'The woman who fits into the picture of Millie Pink as we know her could not have written that letter!'

'Either she did not write the letter, or—but what do you mean?'

'Men can never understand women,' said Joan with a gesture of slight exasperation. 'I am sure that Millie Pink wrote that letter. But the person who wrote that is not the Millie Pink I have met, and you have met. Either the woman who wrote that love-letter is the genuine article, or the tone of it is a pose adopted by the plain, nondescript, confused, untidy, hysterical woman we both know. Well, I tell you, Inspector, that such a thing is not possible. Take another look at the letter. You'll find no confusion about it, no trace of a wandering brain, compact neatness instead of slovenliness, meticulously straight lines written by a woman who screws her hair into a sublime mess, and even forgets to fasten buttons on her frocks. It just doesn't fit.'

'I'm beginning to see what you mean. And where does all this get us?'

'It means this: The person with a brain, with cool intelligence, instinct for neatness, taste for good balance, effective flow of words could, with a terrific effort, adopt the role of a person with all the characteristics of Millie Pink as we know her. But no person, Inspector, could reverse that procedure. In other words, the Millie Pink we know is a fraud through and through, a consummate actress who has led all people connected with her right up the garden path. And that is precisely what she intended to do. Millie Pink, if I am right, has got more brain than all the inhabitants of this district added together. That woman is the exact opposite of everything you've ever thought about her. Now tell me whether I should have opened that letter.'

'I've got something else to do at the moment,' said Billingham, rising from his chair. 'Please get back to the house and keep an eye on the woman until I arrive. I won't be very long. In the meantime, thanks so much for bringing this letter. It looks as though there are possibilities. We'll forgive you this time for committing a theft. Thanks once again.'

II

Billingham stuffed the letter into his pocket, and within a minute his car engine roared. The Inspector was pressing the accelerator against the floorboards, burning up the road on his way to Fasterly.

As he drove into the small town he looked again at the address on the envelope, and found that it led him to a large, somewhat decayed country mansion standing back from the street at the still-rural end of Fasterly.

A sign on the iron gate, 'Fasterly Guest House', suggested to him that this dignified old building was probably in the last years of a long lease and would soon be in the hands of the house-breakers.

The door was open. Beyond it was a glass door which was shut, and beyond that was a square hall of which the furnishings and general arrangement, though tasteful and good, bore the positive stamp of the sort of boarding-house in which retired army officers and disappointed elderly spinsters spend their final years in the impression that they are still alive.

Billingham pressed the bell at the side of the glass door and went in. The hall smelt of bees-wax and breakfast, and a grandfather clock ticked sombrely in a dark corner.

A maid appeared and seemed disturbed when she saw his uniform. Billingham smiled at her. 'Is Mr James Wheeler in? It's nothing to worry about.'

'Yes, sir. He's in the lounge; I'll—I'll tell him, sir.'

She scuttled away and Billingham waited, watching the door through which she had disappeared. Some moments passed. Then the door opened again and James Wheeler came into the hall. Billingham's first impression of him was that he was not hard to look at. Tall, well-built, young, blue-eyed, clean-featured, well-dressed.

'Mr Wheeler?' Billingham asked.

'Er—yes.'

'I'd like a few words with you. Can we be private somewhere here?'

'We can talk in the lounge, Inspector. There's no one there.'

They went into a large room in which the faded cretonnes and the seating arrangements somehow suggested a sewing-bee, and sat down

169

opposite one another with a brass-topped coffee-table between them.

'If it's about parking the car outside the cinema the other night? ...' Wheeler said nervously.

'It isn't,' Billingham answered. 'I'm not here to accuse you of anything, and your motoring offences don't interest me in the least. I want to ask you about a lady friend of yours who lives on the other side of Creepe.'

Wheeler gave a start and began to blush.

'What about Millie Turner?' he asked suspiciously.

Millie Turner! So she had given Wheeler a false name!

'I want to know all you know about her,' Billingham said suavely.

'Do you, by gad! This is a bit thick, isn't it?' the young man exclaimed. 'What do you want to know about her for?'

'Never mind. You needn't answer me if you don't wish, but if you refuse I shall wonder why, and anyway I'll be able to find out what I want to know from other people.'

The young man frowned and gnawed his lip nervously.

'Well, all right. I know nothing against Millie and I'm damn sure she hasn't done anything that would put you on her track ... I say—nothing's happened to her, has it?'

The Inspector smiled and shook his head.

'No. Describe her to me. Perhaps I've got hold of the wrong girl.'

'I should say that's highly probable,' Wheeler answered sarcastically. 'A description of Millie Turner?'

He leant back in his chair, and looked up at the ceiling.

'She's one of those mysteriously-beautiful women, who somehow aren't beautiful at all and yet make you think they are. She is of average height and build, her hair is almost tawny, her eyes rather deep-set and strikingly grey—almost steel-grey. She is charming and brilliant, one of the most intelligent women I have ever met.'

Billingham gulped and looked hard at Wheeler. The young man was obviously sincere. His voice had become quite lyrical during his description of Millie.

'How does she dress?' the Inspector asked.

'In the very best of taste,' Wheeler answered promptly. 'She's the sort of girl that a man is proud to be seen with—neat, fastidious, dignified, calm. Never a shoe-lace undone or a hair out of place.'

'I see,' said Billingham, feeling a little breathless with excitement. 'She has a scar on her face, hasn't she?'

'Yes, but it's very small, and I think it adds to her attractions. It's like a beauty-spot.'

'But surely,' the Inspector exclaimed, 'her

pince-nez detract from her appearance?'

Wheeler stared at him and laughed.

'Pince-nez? That settles it—you've got mixed up between Millie Turner and someone else. Millie never wore glasses in her life.'

'Oh!' Billingham gulped again. The ground was sliding from under him. 'Well, perhaps I have. But tell me, were you and Millie Turner taking your affair seriously?'

'Oh, rather. We're hoping to be married soon. I'm an actor, you know, but things aren't too bright in the profession just now. Millie is entitled to some small legacy. There's been a lot of legal bother about it, but she's getting hold of it soon. Then we're going to marry and go off to Hollywood together. I have connections over there, and I'm sure I'll be able to break in on the films.'

'I'm sure you will,' Billingham answered diplomatically. 'Well, it looks as if I've been barking up the wrong tree, but I'll have to make sure about it. If you're not too busy I'd like you to come back to Creepe with me and tell me definitely that the young woman I'm interested in isn't Millie Turner.'

'Oh, rather,' said Wheeler, rising from his chair. 'I've nothing to do. I just live here on the little bit I've got. It's nice to be near Millie. I see her about once a week. She's companion to some spiteful old woman at Yowle. Leads her a dog's life, and forbids Millie to bring any friends to the house. Mrs Rustable is the old girl's name. She's about ninety-five, I believe. Do you know her?'

'Er—yes and no,' said Billingham. 'Let's go out to the car.'

They did so.

'I wish you'd open up,' said Wheeler, 'and tell me what this is all about. After all, as it obviously isn't Millie you're after, there's no reason why I shouldn't know, is there?'

'I'm afraid the Regulations,' the Inspector answered, taking refuge in the excuse which always served him well in situations like this, 'don't permit me to confide in you at this juncture.'

'Oh, all right,' said Wheeler good-humouredly.

Billingham liked him and felt intensely sorry for him.

III

They drove to Creepe in silence. At the police station Billingham gave his companion into the care of a sergeant, and went off immediately to 'phone Joan Cliff, who had returned to Whitestones.

'Billingham here, Miss Cliff. Keep an eye on Millie. I'm coming over right away. Don't let her out of your sight.'

173

Billingham walked to the outer office, beckoned to the sergeant.

'I'm bringing a lady along in about three-quarters of an hour,' he whispered. 'When we come into the station see that by apparent accident she catches a glimpse of the man Wheeler, but don't let either of them speak as we walk through. If I say anything to you afterwards, take no notice of it. I've seen so much drama in the last two or three days that it seems time I staged one of my own.'

The sergeant nodded, and Billingham hurried to Whitestones. He found both Millie and Joan sitting in the drawing-room. The blinds were still drawn, and death hung heavily on the house. Both women seemed hopelessly miserable. The Inspector had been pondering over the problem of his opening, decided that finesse was of no value, and played a direct card. Staring at the bespectacled Millie he announced:

'Miss Pink, you must accompany me to Creepe immediately. Come along.'

The woman looked up nervously, and commenced to whimper. The Inspector's lips tautened into a straight, thin line. Joan Cliff glanced at him, and her eyelid quivered with an almost imperceptible wink.

'What on earth is the matter, Inspector?' asked Millie, tearfully.

'A great deal. Put on your hat and coat, and

we'll start moving. Hurry.'

She rose slowly, and walked from the room, dabbing her face with a tiny handkerchief. Joan also rose and accompanied her. Billingham paced the carpet restlessly, balling his fist, and then unclenching his fingers. Millie was no longer crying when she returned, and neither spoke as she walked with the Inspector to the car. Before they had travelled far Billingham whipped round suddenly, pointed to her pince-nez, and asked, abruptly:

'When did you first start wearing those glasses, Miss Pink?'

'These? Oh, I first wore them about a year ago. I had to have them.'

Without a word Billingham stretched out a hand, took them from the bridge of her nose, and placed them in his pocket.

'What on earth are you doing?' asked Millie. 'Give them to me.'

'You can see just as well without them,' commented the Inspector curtly, 'and in any case I'm sending them immediately to an optician's so that he can tell me what sort of lenses are fitted.'

Millie Pink parted her lips as though to speak, suddenly changed her mind, and lapsed into silence. The Inspector was the first to speak:

'Where do you keep the smart clothes, Miss Pink?'

'Smart clothes? I don't know what you mean. Smart clothes, Inspector?'

'I mean the clothes you wear when you're away from Whitestones. I'm sure your boy friend wouldn't like to see you as you are now.'

Millie peered at him with a frightened glance. Billingham noticed, for the first time, that her eyes were vividly and steelily grey.

'Where do you keep those clothes, Miss Pink?' he asked again.

'You're talking in riddles, Inspector. I haven't any smart clothes.'

'You think your boy friend from Fasterly would appreciate seeing you as you are now? Because I don't, and you know damn well he wouldn't.'

'My friend from Fasterly?' asked the woman, hollowly. 'Oh!'

The Inspector took a side glance, expecting to see quivering lips. He was mistaken. Her mouth had set firmly. Here was no hysterical woman, no person with unbalanced temperament and confused thought.

'Don't you think,' said Billingham, more gently, 'that the time has come for you to talk, Miss Pink? I'm holding out no promises, but you're cute enough to know when all the cards are stacked against you.'

'What cards are stacked against me?'

'Mostly the whole pack,' lied the Inspector. 'Talking might help you.'

'I can't see that I've got anything to talk about.'

'Think again, Miss Pink. It's going to be a bad moment for you if I start telling you what I know instead of your telling me what you know. By the way, I've had a very long and interesting talk with Dr Cheedle.'

'What did he say?' asked the girl with dramatically sudden interest.

'About twenty times more than you've said so far, Miss Pink. But then, I suppose he's got more sense than you have, and knows that your tongue should never remain still if it might save your body from getting hurt.'

'Oh, I see,' remarked Millie, pressing a finger-nail against her teeth.

As they turned into Creepe Square the Inspector again slowed down, waved to the constable, and handed the pince-nez to him:

'Take these to Jackson, tell him I want to know as soon as possible what lenses have been fitted. Then report to the station.'

Millie eyed the retreating constable, and shivered slightly. Billingham smiled grimly and said nothing. Outside the police station he opened the door for the woman and led her in.

As they passed through the outer office Wheeler stood in the corner, talking to the sergeant. Millie slapped the back of her hand against her mouth, and stopped abruptly as she saw him. Wheeler stared, his brow lined with frowns, but before either could speak, Billingham took Millie by the arm and pushed her forward to the inner room. She was trembling when she faded away into an armchair.

'Well, Miss Pink,' said the Inspector, 'you can begin to see how things are fixed, and what sort of a position you're in. Time you talked, eh?'

'What have you got that man in the station for?' she asked. 'He had nothing at all to do with it, nothing at all.'

'Nothing at all to do with what, Miss Pink?' asked Billingham, quietly. The woman noticed the concentrated stare in his eyes and shivered.

'Nothing to do with all this business,' she replied, weakly.

'Have you got nothing to do with it then, Miss Pink? Because if you have not you can hardly talk about people who might or might not have been involved. Naturally, I had to collect Wheeler when I heard this story about what you were going to do when you drew the money after Mrs Farland's death. Sort of makes him an accessory in a way.'

'Good God, no!' shouted the girl. 'He knew nothing about it. That's true.'

'Well, tell me how much you know about it, Miss Pink. But excuse me for a minute.' Billingham rose, walked to the outer door, and called to the sergeant: 'Get that statement of Dr

Cheedle's typed out for me, and let me have it as soon as you can.' He returned to his seat. The woman, wide-eyed, bit her lower lip, and fidgeted with her hands.

'I asked you before, Inspector, what did Dr Cheedle say to you?'

'Unfortunately, Miss Pink, I'm not in a position to answer you. I can only advise you to make a statement. Naturally, I know everything about your association with Wheeler, and about the hopes he was founding on the money you told him was coming to you. D'you think he'd have married you if you didn't collect that money? I suppose that was about the most important thing in your mind, wasn't it?'

'Just let me think for a few minutes, Inspector,' said Millie.

Billingham lit his pipe. The sergeant brought in a typewritten sheet of foolscap. On it was a list of public-houses in the area, prepared for the Licensing Sessions. The Inspector proceeded to study it with apparent care, pausing occasionally to nod his head and smile contentedly. Millie looked at Billingham, and from the man to the foolscap. She thought she knew what that page held—the statement made by Dr Cheedle.

'All right,' she said suddenly, 'I murdered Mrs Farland and—'

'Wait one moment,' snapped Billingham, raising his hand. 'West!' he called.

The sergeant walked into the room.

'Grab a notebook and pen, and take down this statement. Millicent Pink, I charge you with the murder of Mrs Emma Farland, and warn you that any statement you make will be taken down and may be used in evidence. Will you please proceed, Miss Pink?'

Her face ghastly white, the scar flaming into crimson, her eyes deadly still, Millie plunged into the statement:

'I admit it. I murdered Mrs Farland. But I'm not going to take all the blame, Inspector. Dr Cheedle did more to murder her than I did.'

'Wait one moment, Miss Pink,' said Billingham, hastily. He rushed from the room, found a constable in the rear of the station, issued a snapped-out instruction: 'Find Dr Cheedle. Bring him here. Say nothing to him. Just bring him to me. I don't care if he's gone to Ireland, I want him here.'

Within a minute he was facing Millie Pink again, smiling reassuringly.

'I'll tell you all I know,' she said. 'I've had a terrible life with my aunt, but I could stand it until I met Jim Wheeler. Then I knew that my life was empty and ruined for ever unless I could get out of that house with some money. You've no idea what I went through at Whitestones. My aunt knew I was an attractive woman, and she enjoyed humiliating me,

180

forcing me to dress like a frump, and be a slave to her.

'She fell ill, and then things for me became worse than ever. I could never do anything right, and I knew that I'd have to hurry if I wanted to kill her, because she kept changing her mind about whether she'd leave me any money or not, and I had to murder her while my name was still in the will. That was the time when Dr Cheedle started talking to me about Mrs Farland. I was meeting him every day when she was ill, and he used to say how badly I was treated, and what a shame it would be if she changed her will before she died and cut me out entirely. We talked about this for a long time, and I began to see what he was aiming at.

'Then one day he told me he knew for certain that in the will then in force Mrs Farland had left me about twenty-five thousand pounds. While I was thinking about it, and dreaming about how happy I could be with Jim if I only got that money, Dr Cheedle started telling me that he was in very terrible financial trouble, and in the hands of money-lenders, and would do almost anything to get out of it. It was then he suggested that we should arrange between the two of us to poison Mrs Farland. He said he would supply the poison, I could administer it, and he would sign the death certificate. It looked as though a scheme like that couldn't go wrong. I asked him what share he'd want for doing it, and he said we would split the money

181

half and half.'

Millie Pink paused, smoothed a tear trickling down her cheek.

'I was very much in love,' she continued, softly, 'and the money to me meant one thing only—that I could have Jim for my own. So I agreed to murder Mrs Farland. That was when Dr Cheedle decided that she should take Sleepine cachets each evening before going to sleep, and he doctored all of them with arsenious oxide. We decided to kill her very slowly so that nobody could get suspicious. At first we gave tiny doses of arsenic, and increased them every week. I got a bit tired of it, because I'd read that arsenic in small doses can be taken to the extent of rendering a person almost immune from arsenical poisoning. I told Dr Cheedle about this, and he said we'd have to carry on quietly for another two or three weeks, and then we would murder my aunt with one large dose. I asked him to let me have a cachet so loaded with arsenious oxide that I could choose the best moment to give it to her. He gave me one and told me that I must never use it unless he specifically told me to.

'That was the situation until last week-end. Then all sorts of things began to happen. First I heard my aunt tell John Farland—that was on Saturday evening—that on Monday or Tuesday she intended to cut me out of her will, and leave my share to Penelope Cheedle. That took all the ground from under my feet. It left me with a couple of days in which to murder my aunt before the will was changed. I wanted to talk about it to Dr Cheedle that night, but I stopped for obvious reasons. With his own daughter coming into my share of the money it was better for him that Aunt Emma lived until she had changed the will. I was placed between the devil and the deep sea, and there was nobody I could turn to for help.

'When he was leaving on Saturday night Dr Cheedle told me that the nurse was coming, that she was enough of an expert to detect Mrs Farland's illness as arsenical poisoning, and that we must at all costs stop the nurse from arriving at the house. He said he was going to tell the nurse to come on an earlier train so that she would arrive without anybody knowing about it, and that he would invite her to visit him immediately.

'He said that once he got her inside the house he'd persuade her to take some tea, and then he'd dose her with so much Sleepine that she wouldn't know whether she was on her head or her heels until she died.

'He had worked things out beautifully. He said that in order to ensure that she remained conscious until she reached a safe spot, he would tell her that I knew more about the case than anyone else, that he had arranged for her to see me, and that strict secrecy had to be preserved. For that reason he was going to persuade Nurse Ponting that I was to see her near the goods yard at the rear of the station about quarter-past three. He told me that by the time she reached me the nurse would be almost asleep, and it would be my job to take her to the ladies' waiting-room on the platform and stay with her until she went into a coma. I knew that there would be nobody on the platform at that time, and the idea sounded almost foolproof. Of course, he wanted me with the nurse in case there was a slip of any sort. She might, for instance, have grown suspicious, and given herself a powerful emetic. It was my job to see that nothing like that happened. It didn't sound very difficult.

'I motored in with John Farland, and he dropped me at the church. I was feeling a bit scared, and pretended to be ill. That's how I got the seat near the door. After listening to the music for about half an hour I slipped out, and got round to the goods station. I hadn't been there more than three or four minutes when Nurse Ponting arrived. She looked very ill, and drowsy. I commented on her appearance, and told her that we'd better sit down for a while. Then I took her into the waiting-room. I talked about the case until she went to sleep. When I was sure that she was safe for a while I took a small whisky bottle from my bag, drank what little remained, and that seemed to steady me. I peeped into the other waiting-room. It was empty, and I left the bottle behind me. I thought that might make things look more confusing. Then I took another look at the nurse, saw that she was hopelessly asleep, and dragged her into the lavatory. After that I took an almost empty bottle of Sleepine cachets—it'd been used by Aunt Emma—and left it in the nurse's bag so that it might look like suicide.'

Millie Pink stopped, almost out of breath. She had made the statement at lightning speed. The words had tumbled out of her mouth in a torrent.

'And with regard to Mrs Farland?' asked Inspector Billingham. He had decided to make no charge against the woman concerning the death of the nurse—for the moment.

'You can almost guess what happened, I should think,' said Millie. 'I was anxious that Aunt Emma should die before she changed the will. I was sure that when Dr Cheedle knew of the change to be made he would not agree to her murder. I suspected that business of his forgetting that the supply had run low, and when the new bottle was brought by Parry I couldn't get the idea out of my mind that Dr Cheedle was trying to double-cross me.

'On the Sunday he had arranged things so that it was Penelope who gave the Sleepine to Nurse Ponting. Penelope knew nothing about it, of course. Cheedle got them both out of her room for a moment, and then slipped the tablets into the nurse's tea. If he would deliberately implicate his own daughter, I didn't think that I could feel confident of him. Not only that, but at that time it was to his advantage to let Mrs Farland live until she had altered her will again and cut me out.

'He came to the house that night. I heard him creep along the passage and I opened my door and saw him. I think Penelope saw him, too; she went downstairs and looked out of the window. I knew why he'd come to the house. He must have learned that the will was going to be changed, and he'd come to remove the poisoned cachets in case I tried to make an end of Mrs Farland that night.

'When I went to the medicine cupboard I saw that that was what he had done. He had taken away the old bottle with the single cachet in it, and substituted a new bottle for the one with the nick in it—the one Dr Parry had brought.

'But I made one move too many for him. I opened the new bottle, took out the top cachet and substituted the fatal cachet of arsenious oxide which Cheedle had given me long before. That was the cachet which Penelope gave my aunt with the Benger's at ten o'clock.'

'But Dr Cheedle was at the Morrisons' confinement at Cobling that night,' Billingham objected.

Millie Pink gave him a long, suspicious look.

'Haven't you broken that alibi yet? He told the midwife he needed some more ether, and left the cottage for an hour; but instead of going to his surgery he went to Whitestones. Well, I've finished, Inspector. What are you going to do with me now?'

'Just a moment,' said Billingham. 'Why did Penelope say that the bottle had not been changed?'

'She wasn't certain about John, and gave him a helping hand.'

'Have you talked to Dr Cheedle since that night, Miss Pink?'

'No,' she said violently, 'and I know he daren't talk to me. Take me away from here. Let's get it over with.'

'Sergeant,' ordered the Inspector, 'drive Miss Pink over to Waling Gaol. I'll phone them when you've gone.'

IV

Inspector Billingham was sitting alone in his office, with a satisfied smile playing round his face, when Dr Cheedle was ushered in.

'Sit down, Doctor,' the Inspector said, and as Cheedle did so, he went on quietly: 'Why did you need the two thousand pounds you borrowed from Mactavish, and why were you so certain that you could repay the loan shortly?'

187

Cheedle's lower lip sagged, his eyes narrowed, and he seemed to collapse in the chair. Billingham watched intently.

'How do you know that?' Cheedle whispered.

'Millie Pink has been talking,' the Inspector answered. 'Here is what she said. You'd better read it.'

He pushed across the desk a carbon copy of Millie Pink's statement. The doctor's hands quivered as he picked it up, and as he read his face blanched. Before he reached the end of the sheets he was trembling so violently that the paper rustled like a bird's wings.

Suddenly he let the statement fall, and he leaned back in the chair with his hands over his face.

'I'm afraid it's no good denying any of it,' he said huskily.

'I'm afraid not,' Billingham agreed. 'I charge you with the murder of Nurse Ponting, and I warn you that any statement...'

'Cut that out!' Cheedle snarled with sudden violence, taking his hands away from his face. 'I know when I'm beaten. Blast the woman! I might have known she hadn't the guts to stay dumb and say nothing. I admit everything in her statement. There's nothing to be gained by denying it. Of course, I didn't want Mrs Farland murdered when I heard that my own daughter was due to collect the twenty-five thousand under the terms of the new will. I met

188

John Farland when I was on the way to Mrs Morrison's confinement and he told me. The bottle of Sleepine I'd left out for Parry to deliver was loaded with arsenic, that's why I had to get it back—just as Millie Pink said. The bottles I took away you'll find somewhere in the River Trell near the third bridge. I threw them there.'

V

It was ten o'clock that night when Billingham walked towards the railway station. As he drew near a taxi came to a halt outside. The slim figure of Joan Cliff slipped in through the open doorway. The Inspector waved to her, and she waited for him.

'Congratulations, Inspector,' she said 'A very nice piece of work.'

'The praise should be reserved for you, Miss Cliff. Thanks for all you did to help me. I'd never have cracked the case without you. When will you come down to see us again?'

'When I get my annual leave—maybe I'll come. You forget I'm a common dispenser, and we work at tremendous pressure.'

'I'd like to work in your dispensary, Miss Cliff.'

'Well, you're working next door to it.'

'I don't follow you.'

'Perhaps not. You see, I didn't tell you what I dispense. I try to earn my living by dispensing justice. I'm attached to the C.I.D. of L Division, Metropolitan Police. And after all, Nurse Ponting was my aunt. Good-bye.'

NOTES
(in a letter to his literary agent)

DEAR MISS HUGHES,

Under separate cover you will find my concluding chapter for the Six Author Story. I am writing this letter at some length as I would like you to forward it to Mr Lees, of Allied Newspapers, together with the whole story. He will then follow clearly what I have in mind.

First, let me say that whoever undertakes the work of 'vetting' the chapters will have to perform the damnable job with phenomenal care, considerable brilliance, and an eye usable for threading needles at ten yards' range! Since the authors have chopped and changed throughout the story with varying suspects each has led differing trails that necessarily involve a number of inexplicable contradictions. I think Mr Crofts' use of the subjective method when dealing with the thoughts of characters should, in particular, be scrutinised with care.

In common with F.T.J. I have abandoned the ingeniously effective tables and plans of

Sayers and Crofts. I imagine the reader is faced with a shoal of massive red herrings without being led through the maze of a Bradshaw, and the intricacies of Crofts' topographical adventure.

It would certainly strike a new note in serial fiction—or any other form of crime fiction—if the authors' notes were added at the conclusion of each instalment. At least it would play fair with the reader by taking him behind the scenes. And it would not destroy the interest, since each collaborator plumps for various clues, and various murderers. That, of course, is a matter for Mr Lees to decide. I merely make the suggestion.

Naturally, any person desiring to alter any part of my instalment is invited to do so. With these few words, and a heavy sigh of relief, I pass the story along. May heaven preserve me from such a fate in the future!

Sincerely,
DAVID HUME.

Photoset, printed and bound in Great Britain by
REDWOOD PRESS LIMITED, Melksham, Wiltshire